Outback Surgeons

*These Outback heroes aren't looking for love,
but in the caring country town of
Meeraji Lake…it's catching!*

Welcome to Meeraji Lake—
where Oscar Price and Felix McLaren find
sharing the doctors' quarters with ice queen
Daisy Forsythe-York and über-friendly
Harriette Jones is the perfect recipe for love…

Find out what happens in
Daisy and Oscar's story

English Rose in the Outback

and

Harriette and Felix's story

A Family for Chloe

Don't miss the *Outback Surgeons* duet
from Mills & Boon Medical Romance author
Lucy Clark

Available May 2016!

Dear Reader,

I have to confess I've had a difficult time creating the town of Meeraji Lake. Small Outback Australian towns often contain a plethora of fun-loving characters, and to put all those eccentric secondary characters into this story would have left little room for us to really get to know Daisy and Oscar.

So I'll let you know that in this close country community are characters such as Erica and Glenys. These two women have been best friends since primary school. Both were raised in rural Victoria, but headed to the big city of Melbourne to do their training. Erica became a schoolteacher and Glenys became a nurse. And there's Bazza, a typical Outback bloke who loves the dust, flies and heat, but most of all a bit of a bar-room brawl on a Friday night. Needless to say he knows Oscar quite well from all the times he's needed stitches in his head or a bandage on his hand.

Tori and Scott are also wonderful characters, both of them not sure whether to move forward or to call it quits. Henry, the police officer, is a quiet, unassuming sort of guy, but when it comes to the time for him to break up a fight or protect the people of his town, this black-belted, ex-Army guy takes his duties seriously. There's Pat McGovern, too, a self-professed hypochondriac who always panics about his health. And Adonni and Bill and Sarah—excellent nurses, all of them—and of course Oscar Price, our dashing hero.

This is the fun-loving, caring community of Meeraji Lake that Daisy Forsythe-York finds herself working in. For Daisy it's as though a splash of colour has entered her life, but for a while she isn't quite sure how to respond. Thankfully Oscar is there to help her navigate the vibrant personalities of this little town, and in the process both of them run the risk of losing their hearts.

I do hope you enjoy getting to know Daisy and Oscar.

Warmest regards,

Lucy

ENGLISH ROSE
IN THE OUTBACK

BY
LUCY CLARK

This is a work of fiction. Names, characters, places, locations and
incidents are purely fictional and bear no relationship to any real
life individuals, living or dead, or to any actual places, business
establishments, locations, events or incidents. Any resemblance is
entirely coincidental.

Published in Great Britain 2016
By Mills & Boon, an imprint of HarperCollins*Publishers*
1 London Bridge Street, London, SE1 9GF

© 2016 Anne Clark

ISBN: 978-0-263-26426-5

Our policy is to use papers that are natural, renewable and recyclable
products and made from wood grown in sustainable forests. The logging
and manufacturing processes conform to the legal environmental
regulations of the country of origin.

Printed and bound in Great Britain
by CPI Antony Rowe, Chippenham, Wiltshire

Lucy Clark loves movies. She loves binge-watching box-sets of TV shows. She loves reading and she loves to bake. Writing is such an integral part of Lucy's inner being that she often dreams in Technicolor®, waking up in the morning and frantically trying to write down as much as she can remember. You can find Lucy on Facebook and Twitter. Stop by and say g'day!

Books by Lucy Clark

Mills & Boon Medical Romance

Visit the Author Profile page
at millsandboon.co.uk for more titles.

For Tori and Scott

You've helped me, supported me and accepted me so unconditionally that I don't know how else to thank you. Hopefully dedicating a book to you is a small way to show my heartfelt appreciation and sincere thanks. xxx

Phil 2:14

Praise for
Lucy Clark

'A good and enjoyable read. It's a good old-fashioned romance and is everything you expect from medical romance. Recommended for medical romance lovers and Lucy Clark's fans.'

—*Harlequin Junkie* on
Resisting the New Doc In Town

'I really enjoyed this book—well written, a lovely romance story about giving love a second chance!'

—*Goodreads* on
Dare She Dream of Forever?

CHAPTER ONE

DAISY FORSYTHE-YORK PEERED out of the window of the small Cessna plane, which was coming in for landing. From what she could see of the patchwork ground below, it was generally different shades of brown with the odd spate of green here and there. They were passing over the small township of Meeraji Lake, although from where she sat there was definitely no lake anywhere to be seen. What she could see, however, were a few buildings, some made of brick, others were weatherboard huts and there were even a few just made of tin.

She gripped the edge of her seat as they seemed to be zooming rather too close for her liking to the buildings. Were they landing in the centre of the town? That was all right with her if that was the case as it would mean she wouldn't have far to go in order to find the hospital. Besides, she'd been in a variety of planes and transport carriers last year when she'd worked with the military and even though the pilot didn't even look old enough to drive, she had to put her trust in him.

Coming to Meeraji Lake hadn't been in her plan but, with the way things were with her family back in the UK, she was more than happy to be on the other side of the world for a while. A six-month respite would do her good.

'Go,' her mother had urged her just a week ago.

Daisy had been in two minds whether to accept the position in the Australian outback especially given her mother's health at the moment. 'Mother, I won't leave you.'

'You have to leave, Daisy. I need to learn to fight my own battles.'

'But Father is—'

Her mother had held up her hand, stopping Daisy's words. 'Your father is your father and always will be. He'll never change.'

'Come with me, then. Just leave him.'

Her mother had laughed without humour. 'Could you imagine me? In the Australian outback? I don't think my nerves could stand it.'

'But they can stand remaining here? He riles you up every single day, Mother. At least consider going back to Spain for a month or two. The winter here is going to be horrendous this year.'

But Cecilia Forsythe-York had shaken her head. 'I made vows, Daisy. To honour and obey your father. He has a busy few months coming up and needs me around to host his work events.'

'Mother—' Daisy had started to protest but once more her mother had stopped her.

'He wasn't always like this, Daisy. In the beginning, he was charming and loving and caring.'

'Father?' Daisy had looked at her mother in disbelief, but the reflective smile on her mother's lips had made Daisy wonder if somewhere, deep down inside, her mother was still in love with the man who had swept her off her feet.

Cecilia had taken her daughter's hands in hers. 'Go, Daisy. Have an adventure then come back and tell me all about it.' Then she'd let go and reached for a bottle of paracetamol.

Daisy had poured her a glass of water. 'Do you promise to call me if you need me?'

'I promise.'

'I've also set up that separate email account so I can email you without him knowing. Do you remember how to access the emails?'

'You've written down the instructions. I shall follow them.'

'Keep the instructions where Father can't find them. Put them somewhere he'd never look.'

'He'd never look in my bedroom.' Cecilia's voice had been filled with sadness and she'd lain back after swallowing the tablets and closed her eyes. 'He hasn't been interested in me in that way for many years now.'

'Oh, Mother.'

Cecilia had kept her eyes closed but reached out a hand to her daughter. Daisy had instantly accepted it. 'I'll be fine, dear, especially if I know you're not putting your life on hold for me. Go to Australia. Find yourself a nice man.'

Daisy had laughed and kissed her mother's cheek. 'That's hardly my main motivation for going, Mother.'

'I worry about you. You're thirty-eight, Daisy. Don't let the past dictate your future.'

'There's more to life than getting married, Mother.'

Cecilia had opened her eyes then, her voice small. 'I wish there had been in my day. Still, if things had turned out different, I never would have had you and John.' She had forced a smile. 'Well, enough of all this. You've had your Internet interview and the hospital in that small district sounds as though they need some class and distinction, so go and email that doctor back and tell him you'll take the job.' And because her mother had insisted—and because Daisy had really wanted to go—she'd done exactly that.

'Well, Mother, I'm here,' she said softly to herself as her thoughts were jolted back to the present as the plane's wheels made contact with the ground.

There was only one other passenger on the plane and he disembarked as soon as the door was opened. Daisy watched as he walked to a nearby tin shed and disappeared inside. Was that the airport terminal? She picked up her hand luggage and then climbed down the small flight of stairs onto the dirt airstrip, the heat almost swamping her.

She breathed in, the hot air seeming to singe her nostrils. Flies instantly started to gather around her and beads of perspiration started to form on her brow and down her back. She'd been warned that it was hot, often reaching in excess of forty degrees Celsius for months on end, but she hadn't expected it to be such a dry, burning heat.

She started to feel dizzy but forced herself to take a few more breaths, trying not to grimace as the hot air filled her lungs. 'I'll wait in the airport terminal while you collect my luggage,' she told the pilot and, without waiting for an answer, she mustered her dignity, stood up straight and headed for the tin shed.

The instant she stepped inside, she realised it had been a mistake. Where it was hot outside, it was sweltering in the shed. There was no one around, not even the other passenger on the plane. The shed contained a desk with an old landline phone, a thick book and pedestal fan next to the desk. Daisy instantly went over and pressed the buttons on the fan but it didn't work. She was just checking to see whether it was plugged in when the pilot walked into the shed.

'Power's off outside,' he stated, dumping his logbook onto the desk. 'I'll go turn it on for ya.'

He disappeared, but a moment later the fan in front of Daisy started whirring. She stood in front of it and closed her eyes, allowing the air to caress her sticky skin. The clothes she was wearing were completely inappropriate for this weather but it had been freezing when she'd left London and she'd chosen this outfit because it didn't crease when she travelled. Off came her jacket and she unbuttoned the top of her embroidered shirt, holding it away from her skin in order to circulate the cooler air.

'Better?' The pilot's words jolted her and she quickly dropped her hands back to her sides and straightened her shoulders.

'Much. Thank you.'

'Is someone picking you up? It's a fair hike into town.'

'Yes. Yes, I think someone is picking me up. Uh…one of the doctors.'

'The *only* doctor. That'd be Oscar.'

'Yes.' Daisy fanned at her face, her mind exhausted, not only from the travelling, but the intensity of the heat. 'Do you…uh…have any water?'

The pilot shook his head. 'Sorry. Not in here and even if there was any water, it'd be boiling by now.' He swatted at a fly, then picked up his logbook. 'All righty, then. I've gotta refuel the plane and get it ready to return to Darwin.' The pilot indicated the shed. 'I wouldn't stay in here too long. You'll dehydrate and if you can just get Oscar to flick the switch on the power when you leave, that'd be beaut.'

'Thank you.' All she wanted was for him to leave so that she could continue to cool herself down. What she wouldn't give for a cold shower and a change of clothes. As soon as the pilot left, she returned her full attention to the fan before her. Surely her new colleague, Oscar Price, would be here soon. They'd flown quite low over the town so no doubt he was aware the plane carrying his newest member of staff had landed.

Fifteen minutes later, she was a bit cooler but her mouth

was starting to get very dry. She thought about changing her clothes but right now the ones she was wearing were sticking to her almost like a second skin and would be impossible to get out of.

'He'll be here, soon.' Comforting words. That was all she needed. The fact that she was starting to get annoyed wouldn't help her overheating problem. 'He'd better be here soon,' she growled between clenched teeth five minutes later. 'Or I may just get back on the plane and leave.'

'Tori! I need another bag of plasma in here.' Oscar Price pushed past two other patients who had come into Meeraji Lake District Hospital, pointing to some nearby chairs. One was cradling her right arm to her chest, the other had a nasty gash on his left leg. 'Sit down. We'll be with you as soon as we can.' There were so many people in the small emergency department it was difficult to get through to the treatment rooms.

'Tori?' His voice was louder, not because he was annoyed he couldn't find Tori, but because there was just so much noise. When he reached the triage sister's desk, he found seventy-one-year-old Glenys, writing down people's names and other medical information. 'Where's Tori?'

Glenys glanced up at Oscar. 'Hello, love. Tori's off with a patient in room two. She asked if you could help her as soon as you were ready.'

Oscar closed his eyes and pinched the bridge of his nose, taking a deep breath to calm himself down. One doctor, five nurses and an ED filled with patients due to an explosion at an unauthorised distillery was not the afternoon he'd planned.

'It's all right, love. Lots of the able residents are on their way to help marshal the masses. Erica's making sandwiches and Ella is making the teas and coffees. We may be retired but we're not useless.'

'I appreciate that.' Oscar's smile was tight-lipped. He *did* appreciate it, but what he needed now was trained medical staff, yet getting doctors and nurses to agree to come and work in the Australian outback was almost impossible. Almost. 'I wish that new doctor was arriving today instead of tomorrow,' he muttered under his breath.

'Did I hear you yelling for plasma?' Oscar turned to see one of the maternity nurses who had come off the ward to help, holding out a bag of plasma to him.

'Yes. Room five. Can you deal with the patient?'

'I'm on it,' the midwife replied and headed off to room five.

Oscar pivoted on his heel and headed through the throng towards room two, but when he opened the curtain it was to find Tori giving cardio-pulmonary resuscitation to a patient who had a newly bandaged arm and leg.

'He just went into shock and decided to stop breathing.' She kept up the rhythm as she spoke. 'As if we're not busy enough. When's that new doctor getting here?'

Oscar was already grabbing the portable defibrillator before attaching the pads to the patient's chest. 'Tomorrow.'

'Darn.'

'Charging.' Tori kept her CPR going until the paddles were ready. 'Clear!'

The triage sister stepped back as Oscar put the paddles onto the pads and delivered the charge. Tori immediately checked the pulse. 'It's there but not strong.'

Oscar hooked a stethoscope into his ears and listened to the man's chest. 'Push fluids. Oxygen.' He checked the man's pupils as Tori gave a quick recap of the man's injuries. With the increased oxygen and fluids, their patient began to respond well. 'Get him to the medical ward. Tell Bill to keep a close eye on him.' Oscar knew he could trust Bill, as the other man was one of the best ward sisters the hospital had ever had.

'Oscar!' Someone shouted his name but the shout was filled with urgency. 'Treatment room one. Stat.'

Oscar looked to Tori. 'Get someone to take this fellow to Bill then help me in treatment room one. I'll go see what all the fuss is about.' He was pleased that the emergency department was now a little better under control, the volunteers doing an excellent job, but there were still so many patients who required attention. In treatment room one, he found a twenty-ish young dark-skinned woman who lay very still on the bed, eyes closed, a fresh padded gauze bandage on her head.

'She was hit by flying debris.' The woman who spoke stood by the bed. 'Unconscious for approximately twenty minutes, maybe more.' The woman's words were crisp and very British. Oscar knew a lot of people in this district but he most certainly didn't know her. She looked utterly exhausted and incredibly hot. Then again, she was wearing a navy blue trouser suit, which seemed to be sticking to her. He focused his attention on the patient.

'How did she get here? Did someone bring her in?' Oscar removed the gauze pad and took a look at the head wound.

'*I* did. I found her lying in the dirt.'

'Do you know her name?'

'No.'

'OK. Thanks for your help. If you'd like to take a look in the waiting room, someone will see you as soon as—'

'I'm not going anywhere.' The British woman turned her back to him and started rubbing anti-bacterial gel into her hands. 'This woman is my patient and I'll treat her.'

Her smooth but clipped words were enunciated perfectly. Oscar stopped for a split second, the chaos and franticness of the hospital around them disappearing. He looked at the woman opposite him, realising that although she looked worn out, she was also clearly determined.

She was quite tall and he could see she wasn't wearing high heels. Her brown hair was pulled back into a tight chignon and any make-up she might have worn had been sweated away. She looked sticky and uncomfortable yet still she persisted. As she reached for a disposable gown to cover her clothes Oscar frowned.

'Listen, darl. Just because you brought the patient in, doesn't mean you can help me treat her. If you have a problem, go and sit in the waiting room and I'll be with you—'

'For a start, I am not your "darl",' she interrupted. 'I'm Dr Forsythe-York.'

'Dr Forsythe-York? But you're not due until tomorrow.'

Dr Forsythe-York fixed him with a glare before opening and closing the cupboards, finding the equipment she needed. 'Well, perhaps you'd like me to come back tomorrow because it looks as though you have things completely under control.' Even though her words were filled with a dry sarcasm, she still made them sound incredibly polite. He also had the feeling that she was extremely annoyed with him, or perhaps she was always this clipped and curt.

'I can deal with this patient,' she continued, 'as long as you leave me a nurse to assist.' When he opened his mouth to protest, she fixed him with a stern glare. 'This is hardly the time to be arguing semantics.'

'Are you dismissing me?'

'Yes. You know my credentials—we covered them during my online interviews. Now will you let me get to work?' The patient's eyes had opened and Dr Forsythe-York all but elbowed him aside, then spoke gently to the woman before performing the basic neurological observations. 'I'm going to give you a local anaesthetic because I'll need to debride your wound.'

'Will I need to stay overnight?' the woman asked. Dr Forsythe-York glanced over her shoulder at Oscar. 'Dr Price will evaluate you and decide but I would prefer it. Injuries to the head need to be monitored for at least twenty-four hours. Your cognitive function is good, though, which shows promise for a full recovery.'

Oscar was still stunned at the way she was just taking over but, then again, hadn't he just been whinging that he wished the new doctor was starting now rather than tomorrow? His brisk British buddy was right. Now was not the time to be arguing.

When Tori entered the cubicle, Oscar quickly introduced them, wishing he could remember Dr Forsythe-York's first name, but a lot had happened since he'd interviewed the woman online and read her impressive résumé. Plus, on the day they'd had the interview, he hadn't been able to get a visual image of her on his computer so, although she'd been able to see him, he hadn't been able to see her, just hear her.

'Right. Well. I'll get back to it.' With that, he left his new colleague in treatment room one to deal with the patient she'd brought in. No sooner had he stepped through the curtain than people were calling out to him.

'Oscar. Oscar, can you look at this?'

'Oscar? I need you over here.'

'Oscar, am I going to live? Break it to me gently.'

Oscar took a breath and tried to deal with each patient in turn. Two steady hours later and he'd lost complete track of his new colleague's whereabouts. He had no idea how she'd miraculously arrived at the hospital right when they'd needed her most but he wasn't about to look a gift horse in the mouth.

As the sun started to go down, bringing relief from the constant summer heat, Oscar and the rest of the staff at Meeraji Lake District Hospital were able to finally slow down, the emergency situation now under control.

'And many thanks to the Meeraji Lake retirees who were an amazing volunteer force in our time of need,' Oscar stated as many of the staff gathered in the small nurses' station. Some sat on chairs, other sat on desks. 'And while I have everyone's attention, I'd like to introduce you all to Dr Forsythe-York who will be working here for the next six months and who was an absolute godsend today.' He started clapping and everyone joined in, showing their appreciation.

'Dr Forsythe-York, would you like to say a few words?' Oscar knew she'd been trying to blend in, to stay at the back of the crowd, but now that everyone was looking at her she squared her shoulders and stepped forward.

'Thank you.' She waited for the applause to die down and wiped a hand across her brow. Although the air conditioners were on, Dr Forsythe-York appeared to be perspiring quite a bit. Then again, coming from an English winter to an Australian summer, especially dressed as she was in long trousers and a white shirt with embroidered flowers around the collar, it was little wonder she was hot. Thank goodness she'd had the presence of mind to take off her suit jacket.

'First of all, I'd like for you all to call me Daisy. Dr Forsythe-York does tend to be a bit of a mouthful.' She smiled and a few people laughed. Oscar, however, wasn't smiling back. Even though the smile was a polite one, it seemed to…soften her a little. She didn't appear as brisk or as starched. It made him wonder whether she used all that pomp and ceremony as armour. He knew from her résumé that she'd been in the army, working in a combat zone last year. She held a degree in emergency medicine and minor surgical procedures although, as she'd assured him in the interview, she was also quite proficient at adaptive medicine, too. In fact, Daisy Forsythe-York was almost too qualified for this job and could easily have taken up a position in one of England's leading hospitals. So why had she decided to come to the Australian outback?

'And Dr Price...I mean Oscar...did tell me in my interview that you were all very informal here.'

'Gotta be, love,' one of the volunteer retirees said. 'The outback is no place for fancy airs and graces. Just plain speaking.'

Oscar continued to watch as she pulled a handkerchief from her pocket and dabbed at her forehead. She acknowledge the comment and continued to say a few more words but he didn't hear any of them—instead he started looking at her as a doctor looked at a patient. Her face was quite pink but her lips were dry, even a little cracked. She swayed, a little unsteady, but shifted her feet in order to counterbalance herself.

He'd seen enough symptoms of heatstroke to easily recognise them. When Daisy swayed on her feet again, bringing her hand up to dab at her forehead, he noticed she was shaking. He stepped forward and placed a hand on her elbow to steady her.

'Tori,' he stated quickly to the nurse. 'Container, please. I think she's going to be sick.'

'What do you think you are doing?' Daisy demanded in her haughty tone, turning crazed eyes in Oscar's direction, but the swift movement caused her to wretch and within another moment Tori was by her side with the container as Daisy was ill. No sooner had she emptied the contents of her stomach than she looked at Oscar with what could only be described as a death glare.

'This is all your fault,' she growled before passing out and landing neatly in his arms.

'Let's find a camp bed for her as all the other beds are occupied,' he said, scooping her more securely into his arms and sitting down in a nearby chair. How was all of this *his* fault? 'Set it up in my office.'

'Poor doc. What a welcome,' someone else muttered as everyone started to disperse.

'Get an intravenous drip organised,' Tori instructed one of her nurses as someone else retrieved a cold pack from the freezer and placed it onto Daisy's forehead.

'Obs?' Oscar asked Tori, who was quickly gathering the different things she needed. The sister checked Daisy's temperature.

'Just under forty degrees Celsius,' Tori stated a moment later.

'Hopefully now that she's been ill, her temperature will start to decrease, but let's give her some paracetamol once the IV is set up.'

Tori continued to take Daisy's observations and, although Oscar was listening to the nursing sister, he was also well aware of how fragile Daisy Forsythe-York seemed to be in his arms. Poor woman. She'd come to a foreign country to help out and now she was sick. She was showing all the signs of heat exhaustion and if they didn't get her temperature under control as soon as possible, then her symptoms would get worse. He knew from her résumé that she was well trained and had an abundance of experience but what he didn't know was what sort of patient she would make. Usually, doctors made the worst patients, which was definitely true of himself. Would it be true of Daisy?

Soon, the camp bed was set up in his office and, like a

hero at the end of a movie, Oscar stood and carried Daisy
to her new, and temporary, abode. Although the doctors'
residence was just two doors down from the hospital, until
her temperature had broken she needed to be as close to
treatment as possible. 'Can we get another fan in here, too,
as well as a few bags of ice and a water-sprayer? We need
to get her temperature down, stat.'

'Why don't you get that organised while I get her out
of those heavy clothes and into a cotton hospital gown?'
Tori stated. 'Go do a quick ward round as well.'

'But I shouldn't really leave—'

'I'll stay with her,' Tori promised before shooing him
out of his own office.

Oscar shook his head, knowing his colleague was
right, but while he did his jobs and assessed the plethora
of patients who were almost causing the small thirty-bed
hospital to burst at the seams he couldn't stop worrying
about Daisy. Why had she blamed him? What had he done
wrong? It would be terrible if the two of them couldn't get
along as it would make the next six months almost unbearable, especially given the small population of the town.
The best thing he could do for her now was to provide her
with the best treatment and care.

It was close to two hours later when he was finally able to
return to check on Daisy, pleased to hear from Tori that
their patient's temperature had indeed dropped but was
still a little high.

'Has she regained consciousness?'

'Yes. She was a little bewildered and extremely embarrassed about what had happened but I told her there was
nothing she could do except to rest. I think she believed
me because when she tried to get out of bed, she was
astonished at how weak she was.'

'Has she been sick again?' Oscar asked as he listened to Daisy's chest, pleased her breathing was now more steady as she slept.

'No. I've given her paracetamol as well as a sponge bath.'

'Thanks.' Oscar waved goodnight to Tori before sitting in the chair behind his desk, watching as his new colleague slept the sleep of exhaustion.

Oscar sat and absorbed the peace and quiet, listening to the steady rhythm of Daisy Forsythe-York's breathing. What a mouthful. Forsythe-York, and yet it suited her straight shoulders, her firm gait, her aristocratic nose. However, her Christian name suited her even better. Daisy. He smiled and stood, walking over to sit beside her.

He picked up the cloth from the bowl of fresh water Tori had replenished, and squeezed it out before placing it on Daisy's forehead. She was still hot but the drip and the paracetamol were definitely doing their job. With any hope, she'd be up and about in a few days, restored to full health.

'We'll take care of you, Daisy,' he told her, sponging her down with a cool cloth. Now that it was just the two of them, he couldn't help but notice how flawless her skin was. Apart from still being red and hot, there wasn't a blemish on her face. He brushed back a few wisps of hair and sponged around the back of her neck and shoulders. It was then he saw the small tattoo, a little daisy flower with white petals and a yellow centre. 'Huh. I hadn't pegged you as being the type of woman to have a tat,' he murmured.

He had the impression there were many different layers to his new colleague. He grinned as he realised he was quite intrigued to discover them all.

CHAPTER TWO

DAISY SLOWLY OPENED her eyes, not surprised she felt a little uncomfortable. She wasn't exactly sure where she was but stayed calm and tried to think of the last thing she remembered. She was in a room, lying in a bed. A low bed, like the camp beds in the huts…but this was not a hut. She was at the base hospital. That made sense and she breathed a sigh of relief. Her deployment would soon be at an end and she could return to England and resign her commission.

As her eyes began to focus a bit more, she frowned. This didn't look anything like the army base hospital. There was no thatched roof, no mosquito net around her, no chirping of the birds outside. Lying still, she tried to gather a bit more information before she would give herself permission to panic. Listening closely, she could hear the sounds of someone else breathing, someone who was nearby.

Who was in the room with her, the room that appeared to be some sort of office? She could see a desk, bookshelves and a ceiling fan above her, whirring around softly. Well, that definitely meant she wasn't in the combat zone.

She thought hard, trying to grasp her last memory. She moaned as a plethora of images flooded her mind. Flying to the middle of the Australian outback. Of no one meeting her at the airstrip. Of picking up her suitcase and beginning the trek into town in the scorching heat wearing the wrong sort of clothing, which was stuck to her like glue. She remembered coming across a woman who had been lying in the middle of the dirt footpath, slowly regaining consciousness. Daisy had pulled out the small first-aid kit from her hand luggage and applied a bandage to the woman's forehead in order to try and stem the bleeding. Then the two women had staggered arm in arm towards the hospital, Daisy still pulling her suitcase behind her. As far as initiations into a new culture went, this one had been pretty horrid.

If that hadn't been enough for her to handle, when they'd arrived at the hospital, it had been to find it in the grip of an emergency, which at least provided her with a possible explanation as to why no one had been there to meet her plane. Where she'd found the strength to push on, to offer her assistance, she had no clue but once the emergency had been brought under control, she'd started feeling incredibly dizzy. She'd started to perspire again, even though the hospital was air-conditioned. Then, to her absolute horror, her new colleague, the annoying Oscar, had singled her out and introduced her. That was when the shaking had started, her body protesting that she was asking even more from it…and then…and then…

'Oh, no.' She tried to speak but the words simply came out gurgled and it was then she realised her mouth was excessively dry. She needed water. She should get up and get herself a drink but the instant she tried to move, she felt shooting pains pierce her skull, causing it to pound with an excruciating pain.

'It's OK. Just lie still.' A deep, soothing voice washed over her and a moment later she felt a cool cloth placed on her forehead. 'Good to see you're awake, Dr Forsythe-York.'

'Why—?' Her words dried in her throat as she tried to

look around the room. She saw the drip, the tube going down into her arm. There were also several pedestal fans whirring around her, cooling the air almost to the point of freezing—yet she didn't feel at all cold. In fact, she still felt incredibly hot. She tried to swallow but her mouth remained dry. Thankfully, her new colleague was beside her in an instant, holding out a spoonful of ice chips.

'Here. This will help.'

Feeling utterly humiliated that she had to accept his help, especially as he had to feed her, she sucked on the ice chips, closing her eyes so she didn't have to look at him. Her first impressions of Oscar Price weren't at all flattering and she knew that if someone had met her at the airstrip then she wouldn't be lying here in this bed being fed ice chips.

'Why do I have a drip?' Her tone sounded haughty and ungrateful.

'You got heatstroke,' Oscar stated. There was no humour in his tone, merely concern. Well, she didn't want his concern. She just wanted to go to her new residence, have a shower and sleep.

'If you're in pain,' he continued, 'let me know and I'll give you some more paracetamol.'

'I don't want anything,' she tried to argue, tried to open her eyes, but the instant she raised her voice just a touch the pounding in her head became worse.

'Good thing it's not about what you want but rather what analgesics your admitting doctor prescribes, so shush. You're not a doctor at the moment, you're a patient—*my* patient.'

He didn't sound smug, as she'd thought he might, given that he most definitely had the upper hand in this situation, but instead he seemed to be genuinely concerned about her. How sick had she been?

'What's my temperature?' Her words were soft but she was pleased that her vocal cords seemed to be working properly again.

'Finally back down to normal. It was bordering on forty.' She could hear him moving around and realised that he was adding the liquid paracetamol to the drip.

'Celsius? That's—'

'Well over one hundred in Fahrenheit,' he finished. 'It broke only a few hours ago, so you'll need to take it easy for the next few days, give yourself some time to recover.'

'But I can't.'

'But you will.' This time there was a firmness to his tone that brooked no argument. 'I was wondering what sort of patient you would make.'

'And?' She risked opening one eye and found that at least the room wasn't spinning any more.

He chuckled then, a nice, warm, rich sound, which she realised she liked. Odd, especially as she didn't know him all that well. 'You're a lot like me. Bellyaching and miserable.'

'I'm not miserable,' she instantly contradicted. 'I'm uncomfortable.'

'In the bed? In the room? With me?'

Daisy felt quite ridiculous arguing with him when she was lying supine and he was all but towering over her as he took her blood pressure. 'Or all of the above.'

'That's right. I remember you saying, just before you passed out, that you blamed me for everything.'

She thought for a moment, trying to recall if she'd actually said that. She'd definitely been blaming him in her mind but she couldn't remember saying the words out loud. Clearly she had.

'Well…I do.' With that, she closed her eyes once more, unable to believe how exhausted she was.

She heard him chuckle once more, the sound relaxing her. 'Lucky for you, I don't argue with my patients.' He pressed a cold cloth to her forehead and she relaxed even more. 'Rest, Dr Daisy. Everything will be fine.'

Would it though? She'd travelled to the other side of the world when she probably should have stayed home with her mother. Would her brother support her mother? Help her? Would her father be his charming self, or his dark inner self? Would she be able to recover from this sudden onset of illness or was she going to be unable to work in her new job for the next week or two? Oscar had said that she'd need at least a few days' rest and clearly he'd dealt with heatstroke patients more than she had so she had no real option but to believe him. Right now, all she could do was to sleep and give her body time to recover.

The next time she awoke, there was daylight trying to peek around the edges of the blinds. She listened carefully but this time she couldn't hear sounds of anyone else in the room. Gingerly, she tried to sit up, pleased when her head didn't instantly pound. As the cotton sheet slipped down Daisy realised she was wearing a hospital gown.

How had she changed? When had she changed? She couldn't remember. The door to the room opened and Oscar came into the room.

'You're awake again. How are you feeling?' He instantly reached for her wrist and took her pulse before picking up the tympanic thermometer that she hadn't realised was on the small table next to her and checked her temperature. 'Still within normal limits. Any pain?'

'My pain is well within normal parameters.' There was a briskness to her words but she didn't apologise for them. 'How did I get into this hospital gown? How long have I been here? Did you undress me?'

A concerned look crossed Oscar's face at her questions.

'Do you remember waking up before? About eight hours ago? It was around three o'clock in the morning. We had a lovely conversation.'

His words confused her and she lay back down, pulling the cotton sheet up around her chin. 'I don't remember.'

'That's perfectly normal. Your body has been through quite a lot. You're exhausted.' He checked her blood pressure and nodded, clearly satisfied with the results. 'And as to undressing you…' He slowly shook his head. 'Tori, our senior nurse, took care of you.'

'Where are my clothes? My suitcase?' Oscar picked up some more pillows and gently leaned her forward before placing them behind her head. 'Thank you,' she murmured, appreciating his thoughtful bedside manner. Now at least she could sit up and talk to him without feeling too achy.

'Your suitcase and hand luggage are at the doctors' residence. I'll take you over later today once you've been off the drip for a while and I'm satisfied you're doing better.'

'Or we could go over now,' she prompted. 'After all, I can take care of myself.' She moved in the bed and only then realised she also had a catheter in. Why hadn't she felt that before? She glared at Oscar once more as though he were solely to blame for her present predicament. It didn't matter that she'd obviously been quite ill and dehydrated, otherwise she would have neither the drip nor the catheter.

'I know you blame me for your present predicament,' he said, uncannily echoing her thoughts and sitting down comfortably in the chair that was by the bed. Had her face conveyed her annoyance? 'However, once you've recovered from your jet lag and the heatstroke, I'm sure you'll see things differently.'

'Perhaps my annoyance has nothing to do with either of those factors and everything to do with being left stranded at an airport, which is nothing more than a tin shed, in the middle of the Australian outback.' She didn't raise her voice as she spoke but her words were clipped and controlled.

He thought on this for a moment, then rubbed his jaw. 'Fair enough.' He smiled at her and leaned forward in his chair. 'But I reserve the right to argue my corner...when you're fully recovered, of course.' Then before she could say another word, he stood and headed towards the door. 'I'll get one of the nurses to come and remove your drip and catheter. Once I've done my rounds, I'll take you home where you'll be prescribed lots of fluids and bed rest for the next few days.'

'I'm not one hundred per cent sure I agree with your diagnosis.'

'You can disagree all you like, so long as you do as you're told.'

'And if I don't?' She couldn't help it. His dictatorial nature was starting to grate on her nerves. She knew it was only because her father was an arrogant, high-handed man and that tone, that 'I'm better than you' tone, made her jaw clench and her insides bristle.

'Then I'll organise a roster of our retirees to stand guard over you so don't fight me on this.'

It didn't matter that she knew he was right, that she needed to rest, that it was the most sensible thing to do— her stubbornness, the one thing her father had always disliked, came to the fore. 'I'm a fast healer so I'll be fine to start work tomorrow. One good night's sleep and I'll be as right as rain.'

'I don't care. What I *do* care about is the smooth running of this hospital and, as hospital director, as well as *your* admitting doctor, my prescription is fluids and bed rest for the next two days. If you're stubborn and come to work before then, I will fire you.'

'What?' Daisy spluttered. 'You'll *fire* me if I recover faster than you presume?'

Oscar fixed her with a firm stare before shaking his head. 'You seem intent on arguing with me, Dr Daisy, and that is definitely not going to aid your recovery.' With an indulgent smile, as though he were humouring a child, he opened his office door. 'I'll send one of the nurses to help you.' Oscar closed the door behind him, then sighed. He made his way to the nurses' station where Tori was sitting writing up notes.

'How's the VIP patient?'

'Annoyed with me for some reason.' He sat on the edge of the desk. 'I think she blames me for leaving her at the airstrip yesterday.'

'But she wasn't due to arrive until today.'

'Dates have clearly been mixed up.' He shrugged. 'Can you remove her drip and catheter, and I'll take her over to the residence once I've finished doing a ward round?'

'Does she need a change of clothes? She might feel more comfortable heading out of the hospital in her own clothing.'

'Good thinking.'

'I'm almost done with my shift here so why don't I pop over and get her something to wear? Did you want me to stay and help get her settled in? After all, you do still have a clinic to get through this afternoon.'

'If you don't mind, Tori, that would be great.' For some reason, Oscar was a little concerned at leaving Daisy on her own. He knew she was a doctor and that she was more than capable of looking after herself, but it was *because* she was a doctor that he didn't want to leave her by herself. She would push herself too far, too fast and that was the last thing any of them needed. 'Hang on. Weren't you and Scotty supposed to be going out on a date tonight?'

Tori grimaced, then shrugged.

'Oh, no. Have you two broken up again?'

Tori looked as though she was going to cry but she quickly pulled herself together. 'I'll go get Daisy sorted out.'

'Scotty will come around. He's crazy about you.'

'He's crazy all right,' she snorted before walking down the corridor. Oscar shook his head, glad he wasn't involved with anyone. He'd had his fair share of relationship failures and he certainly didn't want any more. One busted marriage, one aborted engagement. Yep. He was more than happy to devote himself to his career for a while. Sure, he wanted to have a family one day but there were more than enough children in the district regularly visiting him and the midwives in the clinics to help keep that paternal instinct at bay.

'Life doesn't always turn out the way you expect it to,' he murmured to himself, remembering how his sister, Lucinda, used to say that to him all the time. She was the reason he'd first come to live in Meeraji Lake. She'd looked after him when their parents had passed away in a car accident and he'd looked after her as she'd wasted away from cancer. It had been almost a year since her death and there wasn't a day when he didn't think of her.

He completed his ward round, managing to discharge several patients from yesterday's emergency, and then headed back to his office, pleasantly surprised to find Daisy sitting up in the chair, dressed in her own clothes. The dress was cornflower blue with small yellow daisies on it. Her hair was still up but not in the harsh chignon she'd worn yesterday but, instead, a simple high ponytail. She looked seventy per cent better than before and her statement at being a fast healer flitted through his mind. Perhaps she was.

'Where's Tori?' he asked.

'She said she was going over to the doctors' residence to make sure the air conditioner was on and the fans were whirring.'

'Good.' He handed her a cold bottle of iced tea. 'I snagged this from the fridge on my way here. You need to keep your fluids up.'

Daisy thanked him and accepted the drink, then read the ingredient label on the side. 'There's no tea in this.' She sighed. 'What I wouldn't give for a nice, proper cup of English tea.'

'No hot drinks for you at the moment,' he added as he lifted one of her wrists and checked her pulse. 'Normal. Good.' He pointed to the drink. 'Besides, this variety has electrolytes in it and we need to keep you hydrated as best we can.' He picked up the thermometer and took her temperature. 'Normal. Good,' he repeated.

'But having a cup of tea *will* cool me down,' she protested.

'You're a feisty little thing, aren't you?' he stated and she raised one eyebrow in his direction.

'I'm hardly "little".'

'Anyone shorter than me is little.'

'And that's not at all an arrogant comment,' she retorted, unable to keep the dryness from her tone. She was tired, annoyed and frustrated but she still braced herself for his retort, knowing she was being completely rude but seemingly unable to stop herself. Then, much to her utter surprise, Oscar started to laugh.

The sound was deep, rich and washed over her like a cool breeze on a hot Australian summer's day. It caused a mass of tingles to flood her entire body and her shoulders to relax a little. When he looked her way, she could see the mirth in his eyes.

'Are you laughing at me or with me?' she asked, which, for a moment, just made him laugh a little harder.

'Definitely *with* you. This whole situation, you arriving a day early, the explosion and the hospital being inundated yesterday, you getting sick—everything—there's no way any of it could have been planned. It's just one of those things and all we can do is to shrug our shoulders and get on with things.'

Before she could reply, he jerked a thumb over his shoulder towards the door. 'I'll just go get a wheelchair and then we can leave.'

'I don't need a wheelchair to walk out to the car. I can cope.'

'And that's great. I like this independent spirit of yours. However, we're not going to be driving the car because it's much easier to walk, hence the wheelchair because, for you at the moment, I don't even want you walking that far in the heat.'

'Walking? Where is it?'

'Two doors up from the hospital. The GP clinic rooms are in the middle.'

'So it goes hospital, GP clinics and then doctors' residence?'

'Yes.'

'Where do you live? In the next house or across the street?'

'I live in the doctors' residence,' he stated.

'There are two of them, I get that, but where is your place situated?'

'In the doctors' residence,' he said again. 'I'll just go get you that wheelchair.' He opened the door then stopped. 'Oh, and you look good. Comfortable.' He winked at her. 'We'll make an honorary Aussie out of you yet.'

Why had he winked at her? She wished he hadn't because it had certainly caused a flood of excited confusion to spread throughout her body. She wasn't used to men winking at her. Wasn't used to the relaxed manner of these Aussies. Besides, she'd probably only responded to him in the way she had because she was exhausted. Her usual defences were down but by the time he returned with the wheelchair, she had herself under better control. 'Are you sure I can't walk?'

'You don't need to exert yourself at the moment,' he said before wheeling her out of the hospital. As they went several people called out to let her know they'd all been concerned for her.

She was touched by the genuine emotion from people she didn't even know yet. She'd been wondering whether or not she'd made the right decision to come here but perhaps everything would turn out well in the end. There was one issue, however, that she wanted to get cleared up right now, as it sounded to her as though Oscar was being evasive.

'So which house is yours?' she asked as both blinding light and heat from the sun swamped her. Flies instantly buzzed around them and she swatted them away as best she could.

'That's the GP clinic.' Oscar pointed as he wheeled her past the weatherboard building that had been newly painted. 'And the doctors' residence is just…there.' When the residence, a brick house with a corrugated iron roof, came into view, he turned the wheelchair towards it and started up the driveway. 'I'll wheel you around the back so we don't have to navigate the stairs at the front.'

'I'm not that much of an invalid. I can manage a few—' She stopped, shaking her head as he just continued up the driveway to the rear of the property. He locked the wheels on the chair before opening a gate that had a large wooden fence around it.

Oscar unlocked the wheels, then pushed the chair around to the rear door, which was being held open by Tori.

'Welcome,' the nurse said. Oscar wheeled Daisy right through the laundry, kitchen and into the lounge room. Although the house had probably been built sixty or so years ago, it had been lovingly restored. The walls were freshly painted, the flooring had been recently replaced and the furniture was quaint and looked comfortable.

'This house is lovely. It'll be perfect for the duration of my stay.' Daisy nodded her approval.

'I'm glad you like it.' He parked the wheelchair beside a large wing-back chair and held out a hand to her. She was too preoccupied with looking around to refuse his help. Tori was on the other side of her and together they helped her into the chair.

'It is a nice house. It's been the doctors' residence for quite a few decades. All the doctors who have worked here in the town have lived here at one time or another.'

She settled herself thankfully into the chair and then opened the bottle of iced tea he'd given her earlier. She took a long drink, delighted at the way the cool liquid seemed to flood throughout her body. 'So...' She rested her head against the back of the chair. 'Where do you live now?'

Oscar raised one eyebrow. 'I live in the doctors' residence.'

'You've said that before, but what does that mean if *I'm* living in the doctors' residence?'

It was then that he smiled at her. One of those slow smiles that, for some reason, made her heart skip a beat.

'It means we share.'

'We *share*!' She sat up straight, deep brown eyes glaring at him.

He nodded. 'Howdy, neighbour.'

CHAPTER THREE

'I AM *NOT* living with you.' Daisy's tone was completely indignant.

'You're not living *with* me, you just happen to be living in a house that I live in also.'

'I'll get you some ice chips,' Tori stated and quickly headed back into the kitchen. Oscar walked over to the blinds and adjusted them so the light wasn't in Daisy's eyes.

'Better?'

'Yes. Thank you. Now will you explain to me what's going on?' She'd never had heat exhaustion before, but it *was* exhausting and she settled back into the chair again and took another sip of her iced tea.

'I'll just adjust the vents for the air conditioner. I don't want it blowing directly onto you.' He reached up and changed the direction of the vents. 'Better?'

'Yes.' She yawned. 'Now will you please just tell me what's going on?' There was exhaustion in her tone and she closed her eyes.

'Of course.' Oscar picked up the tympanic thermometer Tori had brought over from the hospital and took Daisy's temperature. 'Still normal. Good.'

Tori brought the ice chips in and put them on a small

table beside Daisy's chair. 'I'll just go make up the bed in Daisy's quarters.'

'Thanks,' he remarked and sat in the other wing-back chair opposite his exhausted new colleague. 'This house was originally built for the doctor of the town and his family and, believe me, back then, the doctors who worked here often had at least five or six children. Then, years later when times had changed, the doctors who came here were single and devoted to their careers. The town council decided to convert this house into smaller apartments but, instead of making them into fully self-contained apartments, they extended all the bedrooms so they included walk-in robes and en-suites as well as a small study area but left the rest of the house as it was. This way, there are four full bedrooms here and then the occupants share the living areas.'

When she didn't immediately respond, he looked more closely at her. 'Daisy?'

'I'm awake,' she said. 'I was just thinking. It sounds as though this house has been set up like one of the boarding houses that were around after the war.'

'Exactly.'

'Do only doctors stay here?'

'No. Several nurses and midwives have stayed here when they first came to town but people either only stay for a short period of time—like yourself—or they like the district so much, they buy their own residence and move out.'

'When you arrived, was there anyone else living here?'

'Er…yes.' He hadn't been prepared for that question and he most certainly wasn't going to go into details about the other emergency specialist who had been here when he'd arrived at Meeraji Lake. Deidre was a closed book and one he still wasn't quite ready to open again. 'One other doctor lived here and Tori.'

Daisy opened her eyes at this news. There was a touch of hesitancy in his tone and she idly wondered what had caused it. 'But Tori doesn't live here any more?'

'No.'

'And your bedroom is…where?'

'To the left of this room. Your room is on the right.'

'So we live on either side of the house with the lounge room between us.'

'Yes.'

'Do we share the household chores?'

'One of the residents at the retirement village cleans the house but if you want to share the cooking, I'm more than happy to do that.'

She sighed heavily again and took another sip of her drink before closing her eyes and resting her head back against the comfortable chair. The next time she opened her eyes it was to the sound of two people whispering. She couldn't see them but could hear them. The room was a lot darker than before and she realised that the sun had set. How long had she been sleeping?

'Are you sure you'll be all right with her this evening? I could stay if you thought she needed nursing.'

'She'll be fine, Tori. The fact that she's slept most of the day away is good, plus her temperature is cool and you've managed to get some fluids into her.'

Daisy looked down at the glass on the little table beside her, surprised to see her iced tea was finished and so was half a jug of iced water. She didn't remember drinking, or did she? She frowned, recalling hazy memories of a soft voice urging her to drink, or sponging her down, or taking her temperature.

'Thanks for staying with her, especially while I managed to get through my clinic and finish treating the patients from yesterday's disaster who weren't so urgent.'

'I'm awake.' Daisy had to clear her throat, surprised when her voice caught due to dryness. Oscar was immediately at her side, lifting the glass of water to her lips.

'I can do it,' she told him, but he clearly wasn't going to listen to her as he continued to hold it until she drank.

'How are you feeling?' Tori asked, putting the tympanic thermometer into Daisy's ear.

'Will the two of you stop fussing?' she growled and, instead of them being annoyed with her snappiness, the two Australians just grinned at each other. Honestly, they were so different from her other colleagues, who probably would have scolded her for being such an impatient patient.

'Let me help you to the bathroom before I go,' Tori said after showing Oscar the reading on the thermometer. 'Unless you'd rather Oscar helps you?'

Before Daisy could even answer, going to state that she would much prefer the nurse's assistance, Tori was already in position to help Daisy out of the chair. It was only then she realised the question was rhetorical and that Tori had simply been teasing. These Australians, with their easy humour, were very different from the people she'd worked with in the past. Within the British hierarchy in the hospital, she'd always understood her position, and even in the army, where she'd been required to fulfil a variety of duties on the spur of the moment, there had still been a strict command structure.

The natives she'd worked with in the combat zone; the patients in Britain; the way she'd been raised—it had always been clear and defined what people expected of her and yet, even though she'd only been in this country for a short time, she found everyone incredibly relaxed and jovial. And even though they worked extremely hard and offered first-class treatment to their patients, they all seemed to be very happy to do so.

Even as Tori assisted her, and helped her to get changed into lightweight cotton pyjamas, Daisy was surprised at how much the nurse seemed to talk about her own life, telling Daisy about her boyfriend, Scott, who had just called their relationship off for the second time.

'I want to get married and I know he does, too, but then he says that once we're married I'll stop him from doing all the things he loves and I won't. He can still go out shooting or go away for a few weeks to Darwin and go fishing or whatever he wants.' Tori helped her into bed and Daisy listened to her chatter, most of it going in one ear and out the other. She was still so incredibly tired, she just couldn't help it, her eyelids growing heavier with each passing moment.

'What do you think?' Tori asked.

Daisy smothered a yawn. 'It sounds as though the two of you are perfect together.'

'Do you think so?'

'Well, I don't actually know this Scott person you're talking about. However, from the way you've described him, he does sound like a nice, honest man.' Daisy wasn't sure whether her words were slurring or not, whether she was making any sense or not, but whatever she was saying seemed to be well received by Tori.

There was a knock at her open door before Oscar came further into the room. 'How's everything going in here? All settled?'

Daisy wanted to tell him she was fine, that she was healing nicely and that she didn't need him fussing over her all night long, but the words didn't seem to come out and she closed her heavy eyelids and listened to the muted conversation between Tori and Oscar.

Again Daisy drifted off to sleep and the next time she woke the clock by her bed indicated it was four o'clock in the morning. She listened for other sounds in the house but couldn't hear any. Gingerly she managed to get out of bed and go to the bathroom before lying back down in the bed. She'd done her research on Meeraji Lake and knew that sometimes, it could get very cold at night even though it was scorching during the day. Pulling the light blanket over her, she noticed a jug of cool water by the bed with a glass and a straw, along with a sticky note that urged her to 'drink up'.

She did as it suggested and then settled back down, surprised once more at how tired she was. It was then that she started to dream, to see herself floating through the sky, gazing down at the patchwork-like ground below, wondering what adventures were waiting for her. Daisy saw a face forming in the clouds and she stopped herself from moving and peered more closely. It took her a while to figure out whose face it was and when she realised it was Oscar's, she smiled.

There was something about the man that she liked, even though she didn't know him at all well. They hadn't had the greatest beginning to a working relationship but, as soon as she recovered from this illness, she intended to do her job to the best of her ability. She told him that. Told him that she liked his relaxed nature and she was happy to be here.

Annoyingly, he only chuckled softly then urged her to drink a little more. When she asked him if he was going to reply, if he was going to say something nice about her, he had the gall to shush her and tell her to go back to sleep.

Closing her eyes with annoyance, she felt a breeze start to swirl around her, lifting her loose hair from her nape and brushing it from her face. It felt nice and comfortable and once again she smiled at the fluffy Oscar cloud face before drifting back into a deeper sleep.

'How did Daisy cope last night? No problems?' Tori asked Oscar when he arrived at the hospital the next day.

'She slept well. I checked on her every two hours and managed to get her to drink a bit more, which was good.'

'She's very exhausted because she doesn't seem to completely wake up when you ask her to drink.'

Oscar crossed his arms and leaned against the desk, straightening his legs out before him. 'She sort of did—wake up, I mean. Around four o'clock. I heard her go to the bathroom so thought I'd check on her then, save me waking her up, but although she spoke to me she was sort of delirious, too.' He shook his head, a slow smile crossing his face. 'I doubt she'll remember it.'

She'd looked so relaxed, so at peace, especially when she'd told him she was glad she'd come to the outback. For a woman who liked to argue, she'd also looked incredibly beautiful lying back on the light-coloured pillow, her dark hair fanned out around her face. It was an image he wouldn't be forgetting in a hurry. Daisy Forsythe-York was become more and more interesting the longer he spent with her.

When he arrived home that evening, it was to find her sitting up in the wing-back chair, talking on the telephone. He waved to her, pleased to see she was looking even better than when he'd checked on her earlier that morning.

She acknowledged his presence with a brisk nod of her head before she returned her attention to her conversation. Oscar headed to the kitchen to make them both a cool drink and couldn't help but overhear the end of her conversation.

'I am so glad that you're feeling better, Mother,' she

stated. 'Promise me you're not just saying that because I'm on the other side of the world.' There was a pause before Daisy sighed, a deep and heavy sound that seemed to be filled with anguish. 'Mother, please call John. Tell him you want to go and stay with him for a few nights, that way you won't be...' Daisy paused and sighed again. 'All right. I will stop fussing so long as you promise to call John. He's your son. He's supposed to be taking care of you.'

Oscar smiled, liking that Daisy cared so much about her mother. He finished making their drinks and took them into the lounge room as she disconnected the call. 'It must be difficult being so far away from your family,' he said as he handed her the cool glass.

'It is.'

'I didn't mean to eavesdrop,' he added as he sat down opposite her, pleased with the way she accepted the drink without making a fuss. 'How is your mother?'

'Doing all right, at the moment.' She added the last bit in a softer tone and he could clearly see the concern on her face.

'You obviously care about her a lot. Have you spoken to her much since you arrived?'

'Not really. That was the first real chat we've had.' Daisy sipped her drink but didn't make any effort at conversation. Oscar had the feeling Dr Daisy thought she could come here to Meeraji Lake, do her job for six months and then leave, but that wasn't how they did things here in the outback. They became embroiled in each other's lives, they supported each other through thick and thin, through drought and floods, through life and death. He eased back in his chair, settling in for a good old-fashioned conversation with his new colleague.

'You're fortunate your mother is still with you. My parents passed away when I was seven years old. Car accident.'

'I'm sorry to hear that.'

'Thank you. I was lucky, though. My sister, Lucinda, was fifteen years older than me so she took me in and raised me. I loved her so much.'

Daisy nodded and took another sip of her drink. Was she going to ask him questions? Was she just going to accept his words, surmising that, as he'd spoken in the past tense, Lucinda had passed away? Come on, Daisy, he silently encouraged. Engage. Converse. Loosen up.

'She's passed on?' she finally asked and he was pleased to see she was willing to make the effort to chat with him. Many of her patients would want to chat and all that chatting was usually a very important part of general health care, especially with their more senior patients. Even though they were a tight community, many people did still suffer from loneliness. Knowing that Daisy was willing to ask questions, even if she didn't feel like it, decreased his concern about her fitting in. Many people had been put off by the snobby tourists that occasionally came through their town, with their airs and graces, and Daisy hadn't exactly made the best first impression with her haughty attitude. Now, at least, it was good to see she was starting to loosen up…even if it was just a bit.

'Almost twelve months ago. Breast cancer. I moved to Meeraji Lake to be with her, to help her through until the end.'

'That's a difficult thing to do, to watch a loved one deteriorate.' She sipped her drink.

'Have you had to do that, too? Your father?'

Daisy almost choked on her iced tea. 'No. No.' She cleared her throat and shook her head. 'My father is most definitely alive.' She clenched her jaw and he received the distinct impression that she wasn't too fond of her father. 'No doubt he'll outlive us all.'

Oscar couldn't help but smile at the way she muttered the last part. 'He can't be as bad as all that.'

'Huh,' was her only answer, which indicated that she clearly did not agree with him. 'How was your day at the hospital?'

'It was…far more relaxed than the past two days. Clinic is still overflowing with patients but they've all been seen and I get to be rewarded with a coldie.' He raised his glass in the air, then took a long drink, noting the way she'd changed the subject. Clearly she didn't want to discuss her father any more.

'You don't go to the pub?' she asked.

'The pub?'

At his question, Daisy looked a little confused. 'When I was doing my research about Australia, I was led to understand that the main hub of any outback town is the local pub and that at the end of the week people would often celebrate with what was called a "knock-off beer". Is that correct?'

Oscar was utterly delighted she'd taken the time to do a bit of research on their culture. 'That is one hundred per cent correct, but as it isn't yet Friday it's just a knock-off iced tea for me tonight.'

'Knock-off? As in it isn't real? I wasn't quite sure what it meant.'

'It means you've finished work for the week. Clocked off. Knocked off. Time for weekend fun…or in our case weekend sport.'

'Oh? What type of sport?'

'Rugby. Australian Rules football. Cricket. You name it, they play it and we get to deal with the injuries from it.'

And then it happened. Daisy smiled at him. Not a polite smile but a genuine one. Her perfectly straight white teeth, her twinkling brown eyes, her head angled slightly to the side, her low ponytail sliding off her shoulder. The whole picture was one of pure beauty and he was by no means unaffected by it. His gut tightened and his breath caught momentarily in his throat. Did she have any idea just how stunning she was?

'Oscar?' She was looking at him with confusion now and he belatedly realised she'd asked him a question.

'Pardon?'

'I asked which sport you prefer.'

He couldn't think straight, couldn't get his brain to function properly so he merely shrugged one shoulder and said, 'I like them all but I'm always on call so can never really commit to be a part of the team.'

'Have you always been the only doctor here? Presumably before you came there was another doctor here.'

He looked into the bottom of his empty glass and nodded. 'There was. Deidre.' He cleared his throat, not really wanting to talk about his ex-fiancée, but he knew that, as nothing was kept secret in this town, Daisy would soon find out about his past.

'Where is she now?'

Oscar placed his glass on the table, then stood and walked to the window. 'She's in Canada, I think.'

'Were the two of you close?'

He turned to look at her over his shoulder. 'What makes you ask that?'

'You seem a little on edge, therefore it was an obvious question. However, if you don't wish to discuss it, that's quite all right.'

'Hmm.' He returned his gaze to the window, watching as some of the young children rode their bikes up and down the main street, calling to each other and laughing without a care in the world. 'We live in a small town, Daisy, and as such everyone knows everything so you may as well hear it from me.'

'OK.'

He paused for a moment, pleased when she didn't prompt him but instead waited patiently for him to speak.

'Deidre and I were engaged.'

'Oh?'

'In the end, however, she decided she didn't want to get married and left.'

'Just like that?'

'She'd spent twelve months here, her contract was up and I didn't want to go with her.'

'Especially not if you were here for your sister.'

'Yes. Thank you. So she left and I stayed.'

'And will you continue to stay?'

'Yes. This was Lucinda's home for at least ten years. When she first came to nurse here, they hadn't even built the hospital. Even before she'd had cancer, I'd come for visits every now and then when my schedule would allow. I would have moved sooner if I'd been able. It's quite… serene here.'

He seemed slightly preoccupied by what was going on outside the window as he spoke, his words almost as though he'd said them all before. Daisy sat up a little higher in her chair and looked out of the window through the open blinds.

'Do the children often ride around on their bikes of an evening?'

'It's just after six o'clock. No doubt they'll all be called in for their dinner soon.'

'It's six o'clock and it's still light?' She shook her head, bemused by the difference between this sunshine and the dark, winter climate she'd left behind in England.

'And stinking hot. Summer is probably the worst time

for newcomers to arrive from the northern hemisphere. Scorching here and freezing there.' He sat back down in his chair and unsuccessfully smothered a yawn. 'How was your day? Did you rest as per your doctor's instructions?'

'I did. Although what I didn't need was a roster of people coming to check up on me almost every hour.'

'Every hour?' He chuckled at this. 'I only asked one or two of them to look in on you a few times.'

'More like four or five of them.'

'It's only because they care about you.'

'But they don't even know me.'

'They know you've come halfway around the world to offer your services. That's enough for them. Still, I hope you've managed to rest.'

'I have. I had all my meals brought to my chair, as well as a constant supply of iced drinks. Tori popped in at two o'clock and did my obs, pleased everything was normal.'

'I did receive that report.'

'Good. I hope you're satisfied with my progress because tomorrow I *will* be at work.'

'We'll see. Besides, at the moment, everything is quite calm.'

'No. Don't say that. That's a rather dangerous thing to say, Oscar.'

He smiled at her words. 'Superstitious, Dr Daisy?'

'It's perfectly fine if you call me just Daisy.'

'OK, Just Daisy, do you honestly believe that by me saying that things are calm, they're automatically going to go haywire?' No sooner had he finished his sentence than his cell phone rang.

'I rest my case.' She laughed a little and was amazed at how her body seemed to groan with the effort.

'Take it easy,' he remarked, obviously seeing her wince a little. 'As I've said, rest for the remainder of today and tomorrow, remain cool and drink lots of fluids. Then you'll be as right as rain.' He connected the call before she could say another word. 'Hello?' He listened for a moment, then glanced at the clock on the wall. 'Sure. What time will you be picking me up?' Another pause. 'Good. I'll be able to get about four or five hours' sleep so that's just perfect. Do you have all the equipment?' Pause. 'Excellent. See you then.'

He was just about to disconnect the call when he thought of something. 'Oh, and, Scotty, don't beep the horn when you pick me up.'

Clearly Scotty had asked why because Oscar continued with, 'Because the new doc has arrived from England and she'll be sleeping.' Pause. 'Yes she's a female. You knew that.' Another pause, one that had Oscar's eyebrows rising as he fixed Daisy with an intrigued glance. 'As a matter of fact, Scotty, yes, she is exceptionally pretty.' His lips curved up into a smile as he watched Daisy's eyes narrow with indignation. 'I'm not sure. I'll ask.' He took the phone away from his mouth for a moment, then asked softly, 'Are you single? If so, Scotty wants to know if you'd like to meet him in the pub for a drink some time this weekend.'

Daisy crossed her arms over her chest and huffed with impatience. 'Please inform this… Scotty person that I am here in Meeraji Lake to work. I am a medical health professional and I'm not the slightest bit interested in meeting anyone at the pub for a drink.'

Oscar completely surprised her by throwing his head back and laughing. A second later, he returned the phone to his ear. 'She said no, Scotty. Sorry, mate, and besides, I don't think Tori will take too kindly to you dating someone else and why you even broke up with her is beyond me. Tori's amazing.' Another pause. 'Fine. I'll drop the subject. See you when you get here—and remember, don't beep the horn.'

'So that was Tori's boyfriend, Scott?' Daisy slowly edged out of the chair, waving away Oscar's help. 'I'm all right.'

'Yes. That was Scotty.'

'She was lamenting about him when she came to check on me. It sounds as though he's not as serious about her as she is about him.'

Oscar shrugged. 'Scotty's a farmer, an outback farmer through and through. All his training in life is from the land, from his father and grandfather. Sometimes, I think he feels a little intimidated that Tori has a few university degrees behind her.'

'He thinks she's too smart for him.'

'Yes.'

She placed the empty glass on the table then slowly stood up, standing still for a while in order to steady herself. 'Other people's love lives allow us to be philosophers and to wax rhapsodic that we would never conduct ourselves in such a way.'

Oscar grinned at her and nodded. 'Well stated, Dr Daisy.' Now that she was standing, they were almost eye to eye.

'You really are tall.'

She angled her head to the side. 'Stating the obvious, Dr Oscar.'

His smile increased at the way she'd mimicked him and she really wished he hadn't because that smile of his was starting to have an effect on her fragile body. It was only because she was weak, only because she was still recovering, only because he'd been considerate of her, especially yesterday and today…and last night? 'Uh…strange question. Did you check on me last night?'

'Several times. You drank when I asked you to, swallowed paracetamol when I asked you to. All in all, you were a very accommodating patient.'

'Did you…did you help me to the bathroom?'

'I helped you to the door of the en-suite but you insisted you could manage the rest by yourself and you did.' He was instantly by her side as she started walking towards her part of the house, just in case she overbalanced. 'You don't remember?'

'Not really. Everything's sort of hazy. I remember dreaming that I was floating in a cloud and that your face was in the cloud.'

He chuckled. 'A cloudy Oscar. I like it.' When they reached her room, he switched on her overhead fan and checked the air vents, ensuring she wasn't too hot or too cold. 'Are you hungry? I'm more than happy to bring you in a tray of food.'

'I'm actually rather full. Every volunteer who came in to look after me insisted on feeding me something they'd spent all day making. It seemed churlish to refuse.'

Oscar seemed pleased by her response. 'You'll go far in this town, and no doubt you'll be getting a few more meals dropped in to help you out.' He rubbed his hands together. 'Which means there will also be enough for me. Good.'

As she lay down in the queen-sized bed, which was an old wooden frame with matching side tables, the fresh vase of flowers someone had brought her today filled the air with the relaxing scents of lavender and something else she couldn't quite distinguish. She pulled the light cotton quilt, which had clearly been handmade, over her, unable to believe how her eyes were already starting to close. 'You're clearly exhausted,' Oscar murmured softly. 'Sleep, Dr Daisy. I'll come by and check on you. Later,

I'll run you a bath with some bath salts, which will help those muscles of yours to relax even more.'

'That's not necessary. I can take care of myself. I'm almost fully—' she yawned '—recovered.' Then everything went silent. She wasn't sure where Oscar had gone but what seemed like only a few moments later, she heard her name being called.

Daisy sat bolt upright in bed and looked around but there was no one there. She could hear water running. Had Oscar started running her a bath? She quickly walked to her en-suite to turn off the taps, but when she got there it was to find the bath completely empty but the water still running. He'd forgotten to put the plug in. When she turned to leave the bathroom, she almost doubled over in pain. She clutched one hand across her abdomen and reached for the towel rail with the other, trying desperately to steady herself but it wasn't to be. She was spinning around, falling towards the ground, the pain in her gut increasing. She was going to be ill again but when she looked around for a bucket, she found that the tiled bathroom floor had disappeared and in its place was hard, dirt ground.

When she looked up, it was to see the canvas roof of the temporary army surgery that had been set up so she could operate. The sound of a plane droned overhead and she and the rest of the staff in the operating room braced for impact. Thankfully none came. They were safe...for now.

Neglish made a comment in his native language and they all smiled, but for some reason Daisy couldn't understand him. That was odd because she spoke the language fluently—it was one of the reasons why she'd been stationed in this country.

She continued to operate on her patient, pleased she was no longer in pain, but when she looked at the patient's face she gasped and dropped the scalpel. It wasn't one of her usual patients. No. The face on the patient…was her own. She'd been operating on herself. Was that why her abdomen was sore? Had she been stupid enough to remove her own appendix?

'Daisy. Daisy.' The soft, insistent hand on her shoulder forced her to open her eyes. 'Wake up, sleepyhead. You were having a bad dream.'

'Where am I?' The words were a choked-out whisper and she couldn't disguise the terror in her tone.

'Meeraji Lake.' At the blank look he received from her, he continued, 'The Australian outback? You had heatstroke. Don't you remember?' Oscar instantly placed the back of one hand against her forehead. 'You don't feel hot.' He looked around the room. 'Where is that thermometer?'

'I'm fine,' she mumbled, her senses beginning to return. 'I'm fine.' Daisy waved away his words as her new world crashed down around her. 'I remember.' She swung her legs over the side of the bed and sat up slowly. Blinking a few times, she realised that Oscar had brought her in a tray of food that contained a piece of toast, some fresh fruit and a glass with what looked to be some sort of milkshake.

'What's that?' She pointed to the drink, trying desperately to ignore every single aching muscle in her body. 'You shouldn't be giving me milky things. I might be sick again.'

He raised one eyebrow at her haughty tone but didn't comment. 'It's actually a fruit shake with mango, ice, banana and manuka honey, topped up with still mineral water. My sister used to swear by this recipe for hangovers, sunstroke, sunburn, heat exhaustion and just plain old tiredness.'

Intrigued, Daisy lifted the glass to her lips and took a

sip. It was nice and cool and refreshing. She took another sip, a bigger one, sighing as she felt the cool liquid spread throughout her body. 'That *is* nice.'

'Excellent. I've added some soothing mineral salts to the bath and a few bubbles. It's ready whenever you are.'

It was only then Daisy realised the water had stopped running. 'How long was I asleep for?'

'You call that asleep? I call it restless snoozing.'

Indignation pulsed through her. 'You were watching me sleep?' She stood from the bed, rising to her full height, almost staring at him eye to eye…almost. Good heavens, he was tall. She was trying to intimidate him, trying to put him in his place as she had with so many other men in the past. She was doing her best but she was failing miserably. She could see that twinkle in his eyes, his expression indicating he was both intrigued and amused with her actions.

'I was monitoring my patient,' he offered, but she'd had enough.

Clenching her jaw, she forced a polite smile. 'Thank you for the food, for the bath and for your care. I am now perfectly capable of taking care of myself and would appreciate it if you would kindly vacate my part of the house and return to your own quarters.'

'What was the bad dream about?'

Had he not heard her? Didn't he realise she didn't want to talk about it?

'I beg your pardon but I have just asked you to leave.' To her utter chagrin, he shifted his stance to a more relaxed position, still not moving from her room.

'I'm not one of your soldiers you can order around, Major Daisy,' he stated. 'You're my patient and, hopefully, my friend. I'm concerned about you. You won't recover properly from the heatstroke if your sleep is fitful and restless. Therefore, it's best if you just give in and let me look after you, ensuring you make a full recovery, because if you don't the exhaustion you're feeling could lead to chronic fatigue and none of us want that.'

'I *know* the prognosis, Oscar.' She sighed, feeling defeated and still unbelievably tired.

'Excellent. Then I'll be expecting you to eat, drink and then slip into your nice lukewarm bath. I'll be around for another few hours but if I don't think you're well enough to be left by yourself, I'll cancel my hunting night.'

'Hunting night?' She'd been inwardly annoyed at him but the last part had caught her completely off guard.

'Yes. There are a lot of vermin out here, destroying crops, stealing livestock and generally being a nuisance.'

'Do you go out often?'

'At certain times of the year, yes.'

'You're licensed?'

'Completely.'

'And tonight you're going to Scotty's farm?'

'Yes. Why?' He looked at her quizzically. 'Would you like to come one time?'

'Perhaps.'

He nodded, clearly impressed by her answer. 'I'll see what I can arrange but first—' he pointed to the tray of food and then the en-suite where the bath was waiting for her '—eat, drink and relax. OK?'

'Yes, Doctor.' Her tone was meek and mild but filled with irony.

'And that's the most sensible thing you've ever said to me.' He chuckled as he walked from her room and if she'd had the strength she would have thrown a pillow at the closed door. Since she'd met Oscar Price, she'd found him annoying, frustrating and arrogant. She'd also found him thoughtful, considerate and...fun to be around.

Fun. Her life had been so serious lately, had she forgotten how to have fun?

'It looks as though Oscar may help you remember,' she murmured to herself as she headed slowly to the bathroom, a relaxed smile on her lips.

CHAPTER FOUR

IT WAS ANOTHER two days before Daisy started to feel more like her old self, rather than someone who had been through the wringer. According to Oscar the jet lag coming from the Northern hemisphere to the Southern hemisphere was far worse than the other way around.

'Once, when I returned from a few months in the States, it took almost two weeks for the jet lag to settle down,' he'd told her.

The morning after Oscar had gone out shooting, she'd slowly walked into the kitchen to find him resting his head on the kitchen table, a lukewarm cup of coffee in his hand.

'Will you be able to work this morning?' Her words had penetrated his dozing and he'd sat bolt upright, spilling his coffee all over his hand.

'I'm awake,' he'd said, eyes open. She'd been unable to stop the bubble of laughter that had burst from her lips. Oscar's response had been to smile back, clean up the mess then head out of the door, giving her an easy salute as he went. 'Keep resting,' he'd instructed.

Once more, she'd been inundated with visitors throughout the day while Oscar had run himself ragged doing emergency-department work, clinics and ward rounds. It had made her feel guilty as this was the reason she'd answered the advertisement in the first place. 'Emergency trained doctor required for hectic small town outback practice.' And yet there she'd been, drinking iced tea and nibbling homemade biscuits, talking to the residents of Meeraji Lake's retirement village who seemed to have taken her on as their responsibility.

'Why don't you look at it from the point of view that you are indeed working,' Tori had said when she'd stopped by later in the afternoon to take Daisy's temperature. 'You're getting to know your new patients. Most of these people will be on your house-call list and, by the same token, they're getting to know you, to see if they can trust you when you prescribe a certain treatment for them.'

'Are you saying they've been interviewing me?' Daisy had been astonished.

'In a way, yes.' Tori had packed up the portable sphygmomanometer and grinned. 'From what I've heard, you've passed with flying colours.'

Oscar had come home late on Thursday night and, as someone had already dropped a meal in for dinner, he'd quickly eaten his portion, checked her temperature and then headed to bed, bidding her a subdued goodnight.

It had left Daisy feeling a little deflated as she'd been looking forward to having a chat with him, the two of them sitting in the wing-back chairs opposite each other, sipping cool drinks and talking about his day and the patients he'd seen. Clearly, though, he had still been recovering from his early shooting trip.

When she walked into the kitchen on Friday morning, she was surprised to find a bleary-eyed Oscar yet again.

'Did you go out hunting again last night?'

'You mean early this morning.' He nodded, then frowned as he watched her move fluidly around the kitchen. She switched on the kettle and took out a teacup. Clearly whether it was hot or not, she was having a cup of tea. 'What are you doing up and especially looking that chirpy? I prescribed bed rest. You'll do as your doctor says.' He sipped his black coffee before resting one elbow on the table and propping his head on his hand.

'I've discharged myself,' she remarked as she went to the fridge and opened it. She stared into it for a moment, taking stock of the contents. 'As I haven't had any time to go to the market, I'm presuming it's all right for me to use the food provided?'

'Yes, yes, of course,' he snapped.

She raised her eyebrows and turned to stare down at him. 'No need to use that impatient tone with me.'

'Sorry,' he replied sheepishly.

'Clearly you've had little sleep—again. Perhaps it's my turn to look after you.'

His lips twitched as he continued to stare at her. 'Are you volunteering?'

Daisy sighed. 'Volunteering to boss you around? Most definitely.' She returned her attention to the open refrigerator, enjoying the coolness it was providing. Although she was dressed in a cotton skirt and light, short-sleeved shirt, it was still warm, even this early in the morning. She quickly removed eggs, tomato, asparagus, cheese and milk. There was silence as she moved around the kitchen, opening and closing cupboards, finding the utensils she needed, but she could feel Oscar's gaze upon her the entire time.

'You really do seem much better,' he remarked after a few minutes.

'Like I said, I'm a fast healer.'

'So I see.' She was cracking the eggs into a bowl and sniffing them to make sure they weren't rotten. 'They're fresh. Laid yesterday. So are the vegetables.'

'The vegetables were laid yesterday?'

He grinned and shook his head. 'Pedantic this morning, are we?'

'Perhaps I'm pedantic all the time.' She fixed him with a look, her tone dry.

His smile only increased. 'That'll make life more interesting.'

'So I'm presuming the eggs and vegetables have come from the retirees?' When he seemed surprised at her knowledge, she added, 'I've had several visitors over the past few days and all of them love to talk about their individual projects.'

'Ah. Yes. A lot of the residents of the retirement village have a hydroponics area they tend, because at times, being out in the middle of the Australian outback, it can be difficult to get fresh fruit and veggies.'

'They clearly have chickens, too.'

'Oh, yes. They may be "retired", as they term it, but they work incredibly hard providing for the entire community. We have a sort of farmers' market every week, depending on what's in season.'

Daisy was clearly impressed, and as she cut up the vegetables and grated a bit of cheese she could see that the ingredients were indeed fresh. She popped a bit of the tomato into her mouth and savoured the taste. 'Delicious. Much better than getting them from a supermarket.'

'We are spoiled. Of course, the plane comes in daily as well, bringing passengers—' he gestured to her '—and food supplies and the mail. We used to only get deliveries twice a week until one of the local lads got his plane licence and a plane and decided to provide this much-needed service for the community.'

Daisy poured the egg mixture into the pan, then slowly stirred it around. 'It's as though you have your own little army in this town, supporting each other in every way possible. Even down to the local doctor going on a hunting trip.'

Oscar growled into his coffee and took another sip. 'Foxes are vermin out here.'

'Foxes are vermin in England as well, hence why kings and queens have taken part in fox hunts for years.'

'You're not against hunting?'

She looked at him over her shoulder. 'I was in the army. Of course, the fox is an incredibly beautiful animal to look at but they have a vicious personality and will rip a lamb's head off if given the chance.'

'Huh.' He stared at her in astonishment.

'You seem surprised?'

'You're just not what I expected.'

'Oh? And what did you expect?'

Oscar breathed in deeply, savouring the flavours now beginning to waft through the air. Daisy added the vegetables and the cheese and stirred the contents of the pot again. 'I'll make the toast,' he said, not answering her question.

She didn't stop him and soon they were standing side by side in the kitchen, dishing up their first home-cooked meal together. Oscar had also laid the table and poured them both a glass of juice. 'I could get used to this,' he murmured after swallowing the first mouthful of savoury eggs.

'The food or me cooking for you?' There was that autocratic eyebrow of hers, raised in his direction.

'Definitely the former.' He forked another mouthful of the delicious food into his mouth, chewed and swallowed. 'I'm very much an equal opportunities type of man. In my opinion, there is only one thing a woman can do that a man can't.'

'Give birth.'

'Exactly. There is no "woman's" work, or "men's" work. There is just work and the person best equipped for the task should take the lead.'

'Are you saying I'm a better cook than you, henceforth, I will need to do the cooking?'

This time, he couldn't help but laugh. 'Perhaps.'

'Well, then. I think you need to cook us dinner tonight and then we can judge who is better.'

'OK. Sounds like a plan.' He scooped up another mouthful and chewed his delicious food. When they'd finished, she stood and carried their dishes to the sink.

'Leave it. You cooked, I'll clean.' He stood and brought their glasses over.

She turned to face him, giving him her best 'don't argue with me' look. 'All right, but once you've done them you're to have a shower and go to bed. You need sleep, Oscar.'

'But, Daisy—'

'I'll head to the hospital,' she continued, ignoring his protest. 'And take care of the morning shift.'

'It's OK. I can—'

'Doctor's orders.' With one last glare she headed to the back door, took her hat off the hat rack where she'd put it earlier, and headed out of the door, leaving him standing there, staring at her as though he wasn't sure what had just happened. The knowledge put a spring in her step and a smile on her lips.

She couldn't remember the last time a man had made her feel this way. It wasn't as though she hadn't had relationships in the past but most of them had been well-suited matches, rather than based on attraction. During her senior years at a prestigious all-girls boarding school, she'd enjoyed flirting and laughing with the boys from the nearby prestigious all-boys boarding school. Even though the school had organised dances and other combined events, there had only been one or two of the boys who had taken her fancy.

Michael had most definitely been her favourite and they'd dated for at least a year. She'd often fantasised about marrying Michael, about travelling with him and running his charities. Then, in her second-to-last year of school, both male and female boarders had gone on a trip to Asia, where they'd learned how to build houses for those less fortunate. It had been an eye-opening time for her but Michael, although he'd excelled at everything they'd had to do, hadn't been affected in the same way. Daisy had wanted to do more and that was when she'd first become interested in studying medicine. Michael hadn't felt the same way and, even though she'd tried to convince him that they all needed to do more to help, his response had been to sleep with one of her friends, telling her that he was more than happy to keep dating her, to marry her even because she came from good breeding, but that if she wasn't happy with him living his own life, she would need to break up with him.

He hadn't felt at all guilty about the infidelity and it had been that attitude more than the act that had broken her heart. It was then she'd realised Michael had been cut from the same cloth as her father. From then on, she'd kept her distance from autocratic men and instead thrown herself into her studies. In her final year of medical school, she'd met Walter.

Daisy clenched her jaw at the thought of the man, the man who had tricked her. No. She wanted to enjoy this sensation Oscar had evoked in her a little more. She didn't want to think about Walter, or Michael, or any of the other men who had let her down in the past. Right now, Oscar was making her feel light and happy and feminine. He was making her smile, was making her start to relax, and with all the pressures she'd faced during the past few years she needed to relax. Yes, perhaps Oscar Price really was the diversion she needed…for a while.

When Oscar finally arrived at the hospital it was almost midday.

'Sorry,' he said as he walked sheepishly towards where Daisy stood chatting with Tori. 'I didn't mean to sleep that long.'

'You obviously needed it,' Tori remarked.

'If you'd arrived here any earlier, I would have kicked you out,' Daisy told him, her words making Tori laugh with delight.

'Looks as though you've met your match, Oscar. She's as bossy as you,' the nurse joked.

'Hey,' he protested and put his arm around Tori's neck, playfully rubbing his hand on her head, just as an older brother would. Well, Daisy's older brother certainly wouldn't have behaved like that—ever. John had been born an adult and throughout Daisy's childhood he'd kept his distance, often complaining that she was too immature for him.

'But she's only seven years old,' their mother had told thirteen-year-old John. 'She's supposed to be immature.'

'No, she's not, Mother,' John had contradicted. 'Father says Daisy is to attend deportment lessons so she can have that tomboy streak knocked out of her because you certainly haven't been able to control her.'

Daisy closed her eyes as the thought entered her mind. Why had John talked to their mother in such a way? Why hadn't he shown her some respect? She knew the answer of course—because that was how he'd seen their father had always spoken to their mother, in front of their friends, in front of the staff, in front of their children. And her mother had allowed it because if she'd dared to tell John off, then he'd tell their father and then—

'Daisy?'

She opened her eyes and looked into Oscar's blue ones. 'Yes?'

'Are you all right?'

'I'm fine.' She drew in a cleansing breath and smiled politely at him. 'So, clinic this afternoon or house calls?'

'Both. Why don't you help me with the ward round as well and then we can head over to the clinic and I can explain things there to you and later show you how we organise the house calls?'

'OK.'

'I'll just stay here and monitor the entire hospital,' Tori remarked, sitting down in her chair, leaning back and putting her legs up onto the desk in a relaxed position. 'It's a tough job but someone's got to do it.'

With a shake of his head at Tori's antics, Oscar led the way to the ward. It was then Daisy realised he walked very quietly, no doubt a side effect from walking around wards at night in order to check on patients.

It was what he'd done to her the first night he'd gone out hunting. He'd crept into her room to check on her and, although she'd heard him, she'd pretended to be asleep. He'd lifted her hand and taken her pulse before pressing the backs of his fingers to her forehead.

'Good,' he'd whispered. 'In case you can hear me, I'm heading out on my hunting trip. I should be back around six-ish. Keep resting, Dr Daisy.'

Had he known she'd been faking? Had he just played along because he hadn't had the time to get into a full-on discussion with her? A few minutes later, she'd heard a car horn beep and Oscar's quiet footsteps moving through the house. 'I told him not to beep the horn,' he'd muttered before the front door had closed. Then she'd been left alone in a strange house, in a strange town, in a strange country.

Part of her had wanted to get up, to explore, to gather the lie of the land, but the other part had been far too tired. When she'd drifted off to sleep, she hadn't had a nightmare. Instead, there had been a man in her dreams, a man with a cheeky grin, a man with dark brown hair that was slightly greying at the temples, a man with twinkling blue eyes, a man who had looked a lot like Oscar.

After doing a ward round and being properly introduced to the ward staff, they headed back to the emergency department, half expecting to see Tori still sitting down with her feet up on the desk. Instead, they found her doing triage on two young children who had been brought in by one of the daycare workers.

'What's going on here?' he asked.

'Several of the children got into a sand-throwing fight.'

'Ah. Gritty eyes,' he remarked and picked up one of the young boys. 'I have just the superhero solution needed to fix your problem.' The young boy had been whinging and rubbing his eyes until Oscar spoke, but now he stared at the doctor, his little eyes red and clearly irritated by the sand and dirt.

'You do? Superhero solution?'

'Yes, I do,' he remarked, carrying the boy to room one. 'It's called super-saline solution.'

'Wow!'

'He's always been good with children,' Tori remarked. 'So sad it didn't work out between him and Magda.'

'Magda?' Daisy frowned. 'I thought his ex-fiancée's name was Deidre?'

'Oh. It was.' Tori seemed surprised. 'He's told you about Deidre?'

'Not much.' Daisy picked up the notes Tori had written

about the other children with sand in their eyes, checking to see whether or not they had any allergies. It was
all right for Oscar, who clearly knew every child's name
and remembered their medical files off by heart, but she
needed to read up on the notes first. Still, she glanced
briefly at Tori, unable to stop herself from enquiring further. 'So, who's Magda?' And how many women had Oscar
been involved with? If it hadn't been for Tori going on and
on about how much she loved Scott, Daisy would probably have presumed that Tori was another one of Oscar's
women.

'Magda was Oscar's wife,' Tori remarked, but that was
all she said. 'Use room two for the twins.'

'They're twins?' Daisy remarked, looking down at the
two boys who looked completely opposite. Clearly they
weren't identical. 'Right.' She scanned the other set of case
notes. 'No allergies, then?'

'No. Both clean,' Tori responded.

'Right.' Daisy looked down at the two boys. 'Let's get
the two of you sorted out,' she said, the daycare teacher
escorting her and the twins to room two. By the time she'd
finished flushing out their eyes, helped along by quite a
few tears, Daisy returned to the nurses' station to find
Tori and Oscar chatting quietly. Clearly, from the way
Oscar had his arm around Tori's shoulders and how the
nurse was looking rather downcast, the topic of conversation was Scott.

'Everything all right?' she asked as she handed the completed case notes to Tori.

'I hate Scott,' Tori remarked and took the case notes to
deal with them.

'What were you saying about it being interesting to be
a spectator of other people's love lives?' He spoke quietly

and shook his head. 'All I see at the moment are two of my friends in pain.'

'Do you think they'll be able to sort it out?' Daisy asked softly, watching as the nurse gave her complete attention to the case notes in front of her.

'I hope so.'

'Relationships aren't at all easy,' she remarked, wondering whether he'd mention his wife. Had she died? Had they divorced? Instead, he changed the subject.

'We'd better get to clinic. Otherwise, we'll be doing house calls at dinner time and we'll have to turn down all offers of food as you've tasked me to make dinner this evening.'

'Yes. I have, so please, lead on, Dr Oscar.'

As the day continued Oscar and Daisy did clinic for the rest of the afternoon, then headed over to the retirement village.

'How long do you usually allow for house calls?'

'Sometimes it can take all day.'

'All day?' She stared at him in shock. 'You have got to be joking! This is another one of your little Australian jokes, isn't it? Scare the new doctor, type of thing?'

'I'm afraid not. There's at least sixty residents.'

'And we have to see all of them every day? Isn't there just a list of who might be needing medical treatment for that specific day?'

He grinned then and she realised he was teasing her once more. 'So this *is* another one of your jokes. I just want to know how giving me a heart attack counts as funny.'

'It's only because you're so easy to rile, Daisy.'

'Try and control yourself,' she responded dryly, and was answered with another of his deep chuckles.

'Sometimes house calls *can* take all day because we're not only general practitioners and surgeons, we're also occupational therapists, physiotherapists, counsellors and perhaps even a dentist. It all depends on what the issue is, how bad it is and how long it's going to take to transfer the patient to Alice Springs, or even, in some cases, Darwin. It depends on how much it's going to cost and—'

'All right.' She held up her hands. 'I get the point. We're a Jack of all trades.'

'Well, in your case, you'd be a Jill of all trades but that's just splitting hairs.'

'Yes, it is.' Daisy took a deep breath as they walked up the footpath of the first residential unit in the retirement village. 'Let's get started because I have a feeling this isn't going to be a quick introductory session.'

Oscar grinned at her attitude. Even though it might seem a daunting task, he was impressed with the way she squared her shoulders and tackled the situation. Given that throughout the entire time she'd been in Meeraji Lake, she'd been sick, it was interesting seeing her as her normal, healthier self.

As Glenys opened the door Oscar stepped forward and spoke near Daisy's ear, his breath fanning her neck, making her aware of just how close he was. 'Of course, it'll take us a few days to get around to every resident properly. Fun times ahead.' Then he straightened and smiled brightly at Glenys. 'Hello there.'

'Ooh, goody. Am I first on the visitation list?' Glenys, who Daisy vaguely recognised as being one of the helpers during the emergency the other day, opened her door and ushered them both inside.

By the end of the day, they'd only managed to get around to five of the residents and afterwards Oscar insisted on taking her to the pub for a knock-off beer.

'It's all right. I don't need to go to the pub,' she told him.

'But it's an Australian legend and I wouldn't want all

your prior research to go to waste. Surely you want to experience it at least once while you're here?'

'I don't drink alcohol,' she stated, expecting to be questioned, to have to justify herself. She stopped walking and crossed her arms over her chest. After everything her mother had been through, after everything she'd seen while growing up, Daisy was definitely a teetotaller. 'And I'd rather not go. Legendary or not.'

'You don't have to drink alcohol. In fact, I usually prefer an icy mocktail. That's a cocktail with no alco—'

'I know what a mocktail is, Oscar.' She started walking again, slowly at first. 'Do you drink alcohol?'

'Very rarely and usually it's only half a glass of champagne at a wedding or something like that.' He shrugged when she looked at him. 'I've been the only doctor here for over a year now. I don't have the luxury of being inebriated, even a little bit, not when a patient's life depends on my powers of deductive reasoning.' He lifted his arms out in front, mimicking a superhero.

'So why do you go to the pub?'

'To talk to people. To be sociable. In such a small town, it's just like going around to a friend's place and enjoying a drink while you're there. Even the local police officer, Henry, goes on a Friday. He doesn't drink either. Said he's seen too many drunks and what they can do to themselves.'

'Agreed.' They were passing the clinic and then she found herself stepping off the large gutter and crossing the wide road to get to the pub. 'Noisy already,' she remarked, bemused by the number of utility trucks and dirt-covered cars parked in the street.

'Welcome to a Meeraji Lake tradition,' he said as he opened the screen door for her. They found a table and, after she'd sat down, he immediately went to the bar to order their drinks. Several people called, 'G'day,' to her and she smiled politely and waved back.

When Oscar joined her again, he was holding two large glasses with straws and little umbrellas in them. She'd let him choose the mocktails and as she took her first sip she was pleasantly surprised at the fruity concoction. Oscar clinked his glass to hers and daintily pushed his umbrella to the side of the glass so it didn't poke him in the eye.

'Drinking the girlie drinks again, Doc?' one of the blokes at the bar called, the comment being received with raucous laughter.

'You need to get in touch with your feminine side, Bazza. Besides, you'll thank me for being sober the next time I have to put stitches into your head.' This time the raucous laughter was aimed at Bazza, who seemed to take the teasing in a good-natured way.

'Whenever there's a bar brawl, you'll find Bazza right in the middle of it,' Oscar explained to Daisy. He'd leaned closer to her so that she could hear him more clearly. Therefore, when she wanted to talk to him, she did the same, leaning nearer to his ear, trying desperately not to be so aware of his spicy scent or the way his hair was starting to curl around the back of his ear.

'I think it's too noisy in here for me. Besides, aren't you supposed to be cooking me dinner?' She could feel the warmth emanating from him and as she breathed in again she couldn't help the way his closeness made her feel. She felt protected, excited and nervous. These were not the emotions she wanted to have, especially when they pertained to her new colleague. After what had happened to her in the past, especially with her last disastrous relationship with Walter, which had almost tipped her precarious mother right over the edge and incensed her father, Daisy had decided that romantic entanglements weren't for her.

'Right you are.' Oscar nodded and drank the rest of his drink, indicating Daisy should do the same. It took her a few more sips than him but soon the icy liquid was gone. As they stood up Oscar placed an arm around her waist, more to guide her safely from the pub than anything else, and she had to say, with the number of farmers who seemed to be watching her every move, she was more than appreciative of his protective arm.

He dropped it back to his side once they'd crossed the road, then shoved both hands into the pockets of his shorts. It was odd, but right now she wouldn't have minded if he'd kept his arm in place, around her waist, drawing her close.

She had to admit that he wasn't what she'd been expecting. When she'd first arrived he'd been in the midst of an emergency and, even though she'd insulted him several times over, he hadn't been goaded into arguing with her. Then he'd cared for her, introduced her to people and generally been an all-round nice guy.

Yet all the while she had the distinct impression that he was definitely holding something back. He'd talked about Deidre. Tori had told her about Magda and it was clear he still felt the pain from the loss of his sister. Even though she was here to help, she was only due to stay for six months. What would he do then? Advertise again? Would he be lucky to get someone to answer the advertisement? Would he ever leave Meeraji Lake or was he planning to stay here forever? She knew it really wasn't any of her business but she was intrigued by the man.

As she watched him move around the kitchen, cooking a stir-fry for dinner, she couldn't help but notice his long legs, his lean body, his broad shoulders, his handsome smile. Rugged, good-looking and very capable. That was the best description for him.

'I think you're quite adept in the kitchen, Dr Oscar,' she told him as she ate the last delicious morsel of food.

'Thank you.'

'In fact, I'd say you're better than me.' Daisy placed her knife and fork together then laced her fingers and rested her hands in her lap. Perfect and poised, she sat there for a good ten seconds before he laughed and emphatically shook his head.

'Nice try, Daisy. There's no way I'm going to be able to do all the cooking.'

She smiled at him. 'Then I guess we'll just have to share.'

He raised his glass to her and when she did the same, he clinked them together. 'To sharing,' he toasted and smiled that slow, gorgeous smile that turned her insides to mush. For some reason, she wondered whether he was talking about more than just the cooking. Did he have plans to share something else with her? Something to do with... romance? The thought warmed her through and through and, much to her surprise, she realised that the prospect wasn't completely distasteful. Not distasteful at all!

CHAPTER FIVE

DURING THE NEXT week Daisy slowly completed her induction to the retirement village, managing to speak to every single resident as well as being shown the hydroponics bay by several different enthusiastic gardeners, each one proud of their achievements.

'I don't know how many cups of tea I've drunk,' she told Tori as they worked a shift together. She'd been in Meeraji Lake for almost two weeks and she'd made a complete recovery from her heatstroke. 'But I've finally met everyone.'

'Even Mrs Piper was singing your praises in the ward this morning. She said you've managed to get her bumped up on the waiting list for her hip replacement.' Tori spread her arms wide. 'How did you manage that?'

'I know a plastic surgeon who works at Darwin hospital and he knows the orthopaedic specialist.' Daisy shrugged as though it were nothing.

'But Mrs Piper said she's being admitted as a private patient. She doesn't have the money to pay for private treatment.'

Daisy opened the next set of case notes that required her attention, not wanting to get too involved in this discussion with Tori just now. 'I know. It's being done as a favour to me.'

'Favour? Your request carries that much weight?'

'Apparently.' She pointed to the case notes. 'Can you remember whether this patient was transferred to Alice or Darwin? I can't find the transfer form.'

'Oh, that's because they're all here.' Tori handed her a pile of papers. 'I haven't had time to put them into the case notes. I was going to leave it for Adonni to do on the nightshift.' They went through the files, finding the correct form Daisy needed. She was thankful she'd been able to move the conversation away from Mrs Piper's hip replacement as the last thing Daisy wanted Tori—or anyone else in the town—to discover was that she had been the one to pay for Mrs Piper's private-patient privileges. After speaking to Mrs Piper during ward round over the past few days, Daisy had learned that Mrs Piper's sons had both been in the army, had both gone overseas as part of a peace-keeping mission, and had both been killed. Daisy had seen and experienced firsthand the devastation war could cause and, as the money didn't matter to her at all, it was the least she could do to ensure Mrs Piper experienced the best private-patient privileges.

'With me husband long dead, I only had me boys. Now I've got no one, except the people in this town. They're me family now.'

Daisy's heart had been filled with compassion for the woman and so she'd done everything she could to ensure Mrs Piper was not only bumped up the waiting list but also would receive the best treatment from the best orthopaedic surgeon at Darwin hospital.

'I've arranged for Glenys to travel with you,' Daisy had told Mrs Piper after it was all organised. 'That way, you won't be alone in a strange hospital and, with Glenys being an ex-nurse, she'll be able to help you out afterwards, make sure you're weight-bearing correctly.'

Mrs Piper had beamed so brightly, Daisy's heart had

been warmed through and through and she'd slept very well that night, snuggling beneath the blankets as the evening temperature dropped. She was slowly getting used to the extreme temperatures of the Meeraji Lake district, with it being over thirty degrees Celsius during the day but then dropping to three or four degrees overnight.

Back at the doctors' residence later that evening, Daisy realised she was quite content with her decision to spend six months here in the Australian outback. Perhaps if things went well, they'd allow her to extend her contract. She might even be able to bring her mother out to Australia for a few months, to spend some time with her and to get away from Daisy's overbearing father.

With that thought in mind, she rang her mother and asked how she was feeling.

'I'm doing fine, Daisy,' her mother responded, her words firm and decisive. 'Stop fussing, dear.' Daisy closed her eyes and tried to stop the tears from springing to them. 'I'm absolutely fine. Great, in fact. Your father had a party last night and it was a lot of fun. I was the perfect hostess and an absolute hoot!'

Her mother cut the conversation short and Daisy didn't try to dissuade her from hanging up. She'd already received the information she wanted to know. Whenever her mother was self-assured, firm and confident, it unfortunately meant that she'd given in to the drink. Daisy couldn't help the tears that started to pour down her cheeks. It didn't seem to matter how many times she managed to pull her mother out of the quagmire, helping her into rehab, helping her to stay sober, her father would always find a way to destroy the good work and drive her mother to drink once more. Then, on top of that, he'd berate her for being weak and giving in.

When Oscar walked into the kitchen, she didn't even try to hide the fact that she'd been crying, she was that upset.

'Daisy? Daisy, what's wrong?' He was instantly by her side but she was too upset to answer him.

'It's…it's…' Even as she tried the words just wouldn't come. He put his hand on her shoulder and she flinched a little. He drew back, starting to feel uneasy, starting to worry about her. What on earth had made her so upset?

'Daisy? Can I get you a drink? Water? Tea? Iced tea?' What was he supposed to do? He tried putting his hand on her shoulder again and this time she didn't shrug off his touch. He gave her shoulder a little squeeze and offered her another tissue, moving the box closer to where she was for easier access.

'What can I do? Tell me. I want to help you.'

'You can't.' The words were wrenched from her and she shook her head. 'You can't help. *I* can't even help.' Her words were barely audible between her sobs.

Oscar gave her shoulder one more pat, then stalked to the cupboard, withdrew a glass and then went to the fridge, taking out the iced tea and pouring her some. If she hadn't already told him she didn't drink, he might have offered her something stronger to help steady her nerves. As it was, he needed to do something to help, trying to fix whatever small thing he could, and if that meant offering her a tissue and pouring her a drink, then that was exactly what he was going to do.

'It's all right, Daisy.' He put the drink in front of her but when she saw it, instead of stopping her tears, it only made her cry even harder.

'Don't be nice,' she mumbled between sobs and it took him a few seconds to understand what she'd said.

'Don't be nice? Why not? You'd be nice to me if the situations were reversed.'

'I don't know how to handle people who are nice to me.' She blew her nose and tried not to look at him.

'Why not?' He sat in the seat next to hers at the table and brushed some hair from her face. When she shied away, he started to worry. What on earth had happened to make her this upset?

'Don't look at me. I'm ugly.'

He smiled then, pleased to know the response to that statement. 'You are not ugly.'

'I'm all red and puffy and blotchy.' Her words were a little calmer now and she blew her nose again, catching her breath in hiccupping wisps. When she lifted the glass to her lips, he noted her hand was trembling slightly.

'You are a beautiful woman, Daisy Forsythe-York.'

'Don't call me that. Call me Dr Daisy. I like that. I don't want to be a Forsythe-York. I never wanted to be one.' She all but spat her surname then pushed the glass out of the way and slumped forward, resting her forehead on the table, her cell phone clattering to the ground. Oscar immediately picked it up and placed it next to the half-drunk liquid.

'What's happened, Daisy?' Surely she could see he was concerned about her. 'Has someone hurt themselves? Or worse?'

'No one has died, if that's what you mean.'

'I'm very pleased to hear that.'

She lifted her head and looked at him for a long moment before slumping back down onto the table. 'It's just… it's…stupid family stuff.'

'Ah.'

'I don't ever want to have a family of my own because that way I won't ruin my children the way my—' She stopped then, lifting her head in shock, her eyes wide, as though she realised she'd said too much. It was only then

Oscar began to realise that perhaps Daisy's haughtiness wasn't due to her being rude but rather was a type of defence mechanism to protect herself from others. Had her childhood been bad? Had she been abused? There were so many different types of abuse, such as emotional bullying, and often people didn't even know they were victims until much later in life.

'Daisy, it's all right,' he told her, placing a hand over hers, thankful when she didn't shy away again. 'You don't have to tell me anything you don't want to. I'll listen. I won't pry and I won't try to fix your problems.'

'You couldn't even if you wanted to. If there's nothing I can do, then there's definitely nothing you can do.' She dragged in another deep, shaky breath and stood up, scooping up her phone from the table. 'I think I'll go to bed.'

'OK.' He continued to sit at the table but Daisy didn't move, still just standing there, as though weighing up the pros and cons of whether or not to tell him what was going on. He sat still, silent, patient. Then she picked up the glass of iced tea and started towards her room.

'Goodnight, Oscar and…and thank you.'

'My pleasure,' he called as she disappeared into her part of the house. And it was, he realised. His pleasure to have been a witness to that fragile, innermost part of Daisy. He hadn't particularly understood what she'd been saying, or why he wasn't allowed to be nice to her, but she hadn't run away as soon as he'd entered the room and he was going to count this as progress in getting to know her better.

As he lay awake in bed a while later, hands behind his head as he stared up at the whirring ceiling fan, Oscar couldn't help but replay the scene, trying to make sense of it. He hoped that Daisy was asleep, that she'd found some sort of peace. He wanted to go and check on her but, now that she was no longer sick, he didn't have any excuse for being in her part of the house.

Why had she been crying? Her cell phone had been on the kitchen table, which meant she'd just been talking to someone on the phone, but who? What had been said to upset her in such a way? Nothing made much sense only that, by some miracle, Daisy had actually accepted his support.

He knew of old, from his experience with Magda and Deidre, that women often had many layers to them. Daisy's outer layer seemed to be made up of an almost impenetrable hardness but inside…he was beginning to discover pure softness and that wasn't good. It wasn't good at all because he'd promised himself he would never become romantically involved with another colleague again. He'd already made two mistakes—*two!* Not only had Magda pulled the wool over his eyes, but Deidre had as well. Dating the women he worked with hadn't been successful in the past. What could possibly make him think it would work now with Daisy?

After he and Magda had married, she'd stopped nursing altogether, instead more than content for him to earn the money while she lazed around and did nothing. She had often told him that wasn't true, that she was networking behind the scenes, getting her nails done with the wives of other up-and-coming medical specialists. Magda had wanted the high life, the prestige of being a surgeon's wife. She'd never complained about the long hours he worked and she'd thrown great parties that had introduced him to several good contacts. However, in the end, it hadn't been what he'd wanted at all.

And Deidre? He closed his eyes and shook his head. He'd made a right ol' mess of that one. He'd ventured back into the ring of love and been knocked down and out. Why was it he seemed to choose women who had completely different agendas from him? Sure, they worked well, they laughed and they enjoyed themselves, but when it came to long-term life plans no one seemed to want what he wanted.

'And what do you want?' he growled into the dark, and a moment later a vision appeared of the doctors' residence being filled with children, his own children, the house bursting with love and laughter. It was the childhood he could remember, before his parents had passed away, his beautiful, fun-loving mother gone forever. Lucinda had done her best to provide him with a home but nothing had been the same ever again and now even his beloved sister had been taken from him.

All the women he'd ever cared about had left him, in one way or another. Was he cursed? Was he meant to be alone for the rest of his life, just him and his patients? Was he brave enough to step into the ring for a third time? Brave…or stupid? He wasn't sure which.

What he *was* sure of was the dream…the dream of staying here in Meeraji Lake, being a part of the community, of creating a stable and loving environment for his children, cooking a barbecue on the weekend, swatting flies, running around, playing games and all of it with the woman of his dreams at his side. The only problem was, he had no idea who the woman of his dreams was any more. It hadn't been Magda. It hadn't been Deidre. Could it be…Daisy?

'How's everything been going?' he asked the next day as he entered the ED. He'd just finished his Saturday morning clinic and Tori and Daisy were sitting at the nurses' station, going over some case notes.

'Apart from Mrs Piper still celebrating her good news,

it's been fairly quiet,' Tori said, but a moment later the phone on the desk rang.

'Don't speak too soon,' Daisy and Oscar said in unison, then grinned at each other as Daisy picked up the receiver. 'Meeraji Lake District Hospital,' she stated. 'Dr Forsythe-York speaking.' She listened for a moment, then started taking notes. Tori handed Oscar two sets of case notes.

'Patients in rooms one and two just need you to review before admission,' she said. Oscar accepted the case notes and headed off to room one. It was five minutes later when he returned to the nurses' station to find Daisy still on the phone.

'Emergency,' she mouthed and handed him the piece of paper where she'd taken neat and meticulous notes. 'Yes,' she said into the phone. 'OK. So the helicopter...' She paused. 'Good. Thank you, Henry. I appreciate your assistance in this matter.' She disconnected the call and turned to face him. 'Henry's organising the police side of the emergency,' she told him, but Oscar wasn't listening.

He pointed to the piece of paper in his hand. 'Gracie? This has happened to Gracie Penderghast?'

'You know her?'

'I know everyone in the district.'

'I've requested her case notes and Tori is organising the rest of the emergency retrieval team.'

'And I heard you've already requested the helicopter so we'll have a meeting in a minute or two in the staff kitchen and you can give a debrief of the situation. Do you want me to take control of the team?'

'I think it's best given it's my first retrieval and, although I've read all the hospital's protocols, the staff—and some of the patients—don't have confidence in me yet.'

Oscar placed a hand on her shoulder. 'They will do. Things take time.'

'Things always take time.'

There was a hint of sadness to her words and Oscar angled his head to the side as he watched her. To say there were a lot of layers to the woman before him was an understatement. She was brisk, proficient and posh yet she'd gone above and beyond the call of duty several times since her arrival in Meeraji Lake.

'I'll go and get changed into the retrieval overalls and meet you in the staff kitchen,' she remarked before walking away. He stood there, like a fool, watching the way her hips moved, the way she swayed, the way her cool summery clothes made her look less austere than the suit she'd worn that first day.

When she disappeared into the female toilets, which also doubled as a changing room, Oscar knew he needed to concentrate on the emergency, to go through Gracie Penderghast's case notes, to check and see whether she was allergic to any medications and to prepare himself for the sight that awaited them. Gracie. Little seventeen-year-old Gracie! His sister, Lucinda, had been the midwife to deliver Gracie, Mr and Mrs Penderghast having given up any hope of ever having a child. She was their everything, and now she was hurt.

Oscar strode to the changing rooms, determined to do everything he could in order to save Gracie's life. When something drastic like this happened in the town, it didn't just happen to the people involved, it happened to everyone. They were a community and they stuck together like glue.

'We have to save her,' he muttered with determination as he came out of the changing rooms.

'We will.' Daisy spoke from behind him and Oscar spun around to face her. 'Sorry. I didn't mean to startle you.' They headed towards the briefing together but before they entered the room, Daisy surprised him further by slipping her hand into his and giving it a little squeeze.

'You're not alone in this, Oscar. I'm here to help. Whatever you need me to do, I'll do. I just wanted you to know that.'

He stood still for a moment and stared into her eyes. How had she known just the right thing to say? He'd momentarily forgotten that he wasn't the only doctor on staff now. He had back-up. He had help and Daisy was letting him know that she was there for whatever he needed. On a professional level, he appreciated the courtesy. On a personal level, it meant that Daisy Forsthye-York really was quite an extraordinary woman.

CHAPTER SIX

THE SCENE WHEN the retrieval team arrived at the remote part of the Penderghasts' property was not one of hysterics, for which Daisy was exceedingly grateful.

'You'll find that most country folk keep a cool and calm head in emergency situations.' Oscar's words were quiet as they started to gather up their medical equipment. 'They're a strong, tough, matter-of-fact breed of person.'

'Sorry?' Had she spoken out loud or could he now read her thoughts?

'Just in case you were wondering.' He kept his head bent as they left the helicopter and walked carefully towards the patient, who was sitting upright, knees bent helping to cradle her right arm and shoulder.

'Hello. I'm Daisy,' she remarked as she took off her medical backpack and knelt down next to Gracie.

'The new doc,' Gracie said.

'Good.' Daisy nodded and smiled, pleased with Gracie's cognitive function. 'That's right.'

'Hey there, Gracie.' Oscar knelt down on the other side of the teenager. 'Having a bad day, eh?'

Gracie laughed without humour. 'It's not my best, Oscar.'

'We're going to get you sorted out,' Daisy told her. 'I've dealt with this type of injury before.'

'And so have I,' Oscar added. 'So you are most definitely in good hands.'

'Well, that's good because I've almost ripped my right arm completely off,' Gracie said, seemingly not at all hysterical about her injury.

'You're very calm about it,' Daisy stated as she pulled on a pair of gloves and checked Gracie's right shoulder. 'Have you already been given something for the pain?'

'No. I've been injured before.'

'Yes, she has. She's broken her leg—'

'When I fell off my horse,' Gracie added.

'She's had a fractured jaw.'

'When I flew off the mechanical bull and landed on my face.' Gracie even grinned. 'I was almost fourteen then.'

'She's had her appendix out, is due to have her wisdom teeth out soon and has generally turned her parents' hair grey with her antics.'

Gracie grinned then flinched, her expression changing immediately when Daisy carefully touched her shoulder.

'Sorry. Sorry,' Daisy instantly said. 'Now you can add a dislocated shoulder to that list.'

'It's dislocated?' Gracie accepted the anaesthetic green whistle Oscar was holding out to her to breathe in. 'Oh, great. I love these things. They're the best part about getting hurt.'

Daisy frowned for a moment, concern touching her eyes. Had Gracie hurt herself on purpose?

'It's not what you think,' Oscar said as though he truly could read her mind. 'Gracie's just a typical outback kid. Rough as guts and tough as nails.'

'Yeah. I'm actually in a lot of pain,' she said, honesty in her eyes. 'But I knew you'd get here sooner or later. Scotty wasn't going to leave me but he had no reception on his phone in this part of the land. Plus, I knew as soon as my

parents found out what had happened—' Gracie flinched
again and even whimpered a little '—that they'd be worried and so I told Scotty to stay at the house with them,
that I'd be OK until you lot showed up.' She swatted at one
of the many flies surrounding them with her left hand but
then moaned in pain.

'Will you just sit still?' Oscar chided the teenager, a
small smile on his face. 'Look, here comes Tori so you'd
best behave yourself. You know she'll tell you off.'

Daisy couldn't help but smile herself as the nurse, carrying the portable stretcher and other equipment they'd
need, took one look at Gracie and tut-tutted.

'What have you been up to now, Gracie Penderghast?'

'I was helping Scotty out here with the post-hole dig-
ging and got my arm caught in the auger.'

'That's the screw-like part which slowly digs down into
the ground,' Oscar added for Daisy's benefit.

She raised a haughty eyebrow at him. 'I know what an
auger is, Dr Price.'

'Of course you do,' he remarked with a slight hint of
humour in his tone, his blue eyes momentarily twinkling
with amusement. While they talked, or, more correctly,
while they listened to Gracie explain what had happened,
Oscar snapped pictures with his cell phone and took a bit
of video as well. 'I think I've got it all,' he stated quietly
to Daisy and nodded that they could start checking, de-
briding and bandaging the wounds as well as strapping
the teenager's shoulder, getting her as ready for transpor-
tation as they could.

'Anyway, there was a lot of brush scrub in the way and
we couldn't get the auger—' She gestured with her left
hand and was once again told to sit still from both Oscar
and Tori. 'Sorry. Well, Scotty didn't know I wasn't clear,
or I think I'd yelled that I was clear but then I saw another

bit I had to clear and went for it, thinking I had time but—'
She glanced momentarily at her bloodied arm, her hand
almost unrecognisable. 'But I didn't.' She paused for a moment, allowing Tori to offer her a drink of water. 'It's all a
bit hazy and Scotty said it could have been heaps worse.'

Even when Tori put a neck brace around Gracie's neck,
it still didn't stop her from chatting away and it was then
Daisy realised that the chattiness was actually Gracie's
way of dealing with the trauma her body was presently
facing.

As Tori offered assistance to Daisy and Oscar, the two doctors worked exceptionally well together, putting in an IV
line in order to boost Gracie's fluids, performing observations and reporting their findings to each other.

'Aren't you going to put my shoulder back into position?' she asked.'

'First we need to check you haven't fractured your
shoulder, because if that's the case we can't relocate it.
The X-rays will give us the information we need,' Oscar
replied.

'I get to go in the chopper again. Am I going to Alice
Springs hospital?' she asked Oscar as she took in another
deep breath from the magic green whistle that contained
midazolam. Chances were Gracie would hardly remember
any of this but Daisy had to admit she would rather deal
with a chipper, chatty teen than a screaming, sobbing one.

'You'll be going to Darwin,' Oscar remarked.

'Oh.' That stopped Gracie for a moment. 'But only the
really bad cases go to Darwin.' It was then Daisy noted
Gracie's chin start to wobble and her breathing instantly
increased, anxiety reflected in her eyes. Daisy glanced
across at Oscar, read the matching concern in his own ex-

pression before returning her attention to Gracie, making sure she affected an air of nonchalance.

'Actually, you're only going to Darwin because I was the one to organise your transfer and one of my old army chums works in Darwin. He's the plastic surgeon there and he really is the best.'

'So you didn't know emergencies were supposed to go to Alice Springs?'

'Exactly and also because I really wanted you to have the best treatment and Timothy Hartfell is the best plastic surgeon I've ever met.'

'Oh, well, that's really nice of you, Daisy. Thanks.' Gracie's breathing seemed to settle down and Oscar breathed a sigh of relief, mouthing the words 'thank you' to Daisy. She felt so thrilled that she found herself doing something she'd never thought she would: she winked at Oscar, as though to reassure him that everything would be fine with their patient.

Oscar's answer was to smile so brightly at her that for one split second she actually forgot what she was doing, forgot where she was, forgot even her own name. How could he do that to her...and with just one bright smile?

'So how do you know this plastic surgeon Timothy dude?' Gracie asked, her question instantly snapping Daisy's attention away from the confusing way Oscar made her feel and back to the task at hand.

'I know, she's been in the country for the blink of an eye and already she's pulling strings and calling in favours.'

Daisy laughed and he felt as though he'd just been punched in the solar plexus. She was stunning. So stunning, she took his breath away and he couldn't help but be dazzled by this incredible woman. How was it she was able to affect him in such a way with just a smile? Her teeth were perfectly straight, indicating braces in the past. Her eyes were twinkling with such genuine delight as she told Gracie how she'd known Timothy since medical school and that they'd both served in the army.

He tried not to be bothered by the radiance in her tone as she continued to chat with Gracie while they worked. He should be pleased she was keeping Gracie talking, keeping the girl's anxiety under control, yet for some reason he felt a pang of one hundred per cent jealousy at the mere mention of Timothy Hartfell's name.

He tried to push the sensation away, telling himself that Daisy was nothing more than a colleague—a stunning one, but that was all she was. Yes, he liked her. Yes, he found her attractive and yes, he wanted to get to know her much, much better.

Then they could hear a car engine in the distance and as it drew closer they realised it was Scotty. 'Docs, you're here. You're here. Thank God.' Scotty had barely brought the ute to a stop before he was out of the vehicle and racing towards them, dust and flies and the heat of the afternoon starting to descend upon them all. 'How is she? Gracie, honey? How are you?'

'How's Mum and Dad?' Gracie asked as Tori started setting up the stretcher.

'They're OK. I didn't tell them exactly how bad the injury was.'

'But it *isn't* that bad,' Gracie told him.

'Have a little bit more of the green whistle,' Oscar encouraged. They just needed to keep Gracie nice and calm for a bit longer. Once they had her in the helicopter, they could give her stronger analgesics.

'Bill was out and about doing his rounds so I managed to get him on the phone too and he's staying with your parents until we knew more about how you were doing. Your dad wanted to come out here with me but—' Scotty shook his head '—I said he'd be better off packing you a bag of stuff to take to hospital.'

'And you're sure Dad's OK?' Gracie's tone held concern for her father and Daisy wondered what had happened to Mr Penderghast in the past to put such wisdom into those young eyes of hers.

'Yes. Bill's checked his heart and everything's fine. He's not going to have another heart attack, Gracie.'

'Good.' At this news that her aged parents were indeed OK, Gracie sagged against Oscar.

'Scotty, help Tori with the stretcher then tell the pilot that we're almost ready to get going to Darwin.'

'Darwin? She's going to Darwin? She's not that bad, is she?' Scotty remarked but Tori hit his arm, telling him to be quiet. Daisy could hear Tori whispering briskly to Scotty and decided it was best to distract Gracie with more chatter.

'Tell me, Gracie. Do you still ride a horse?'

'Am I an Aussie?'

'That question implies that all Australians ride horses.'

'Perhaps all outback Aussies do,' Oscar added as they finished applying the top set of bandages and strapping to Gracie's arm.

'Then I can tick one box on my list,' Daisy told the teen.

'What list?'

'My list of what I need to do to become an honorary Aussie.'

Oscar chuckled then as Tori gave him the thumbs up that they were ready to get Gracie onto the stretcher. 'If you're going to become an honorary Aussie, Daisy…'

'Yes,' she drawled, raising one haughty eyebrow. Gracie giggled at the sight of the two of them teasing each other, then winced as though she remembered that her body really wasn't doing the best right now.

'Well…uh…then I think we're going to need to teach you how to speak with an Aussie twang. None of this upper-crust Britishness out here.'

'I beg your pardon. There is nothing whatsoever wrong with my accent.'

Tori and Scotty laughed, everyone trying to keep the atmosphere as light as possible so the teenager didn't go into shock.

'Don't worry, Daisy,' Gracie said just before they all got into position to shift the teenager to the stretcher. 'I'll teach you some Aussie words on the helicopter ride to Darwin.'

'Thank you, Gracie. That's exceedingly kind of you.' Daisy glared at Oscar, as if to teasingly imply that he wasn't being kind. He opened his mouth to reply but whatever he'd been about to say was drowned out by the drone of the helicopter blades.

They managed to get Gracie onto the stretcher but as they were strapping her in Daisy noticed that the look of panic was back. She glanced at Oscar but realised he'd seen it, too. With the sound of the helicopter making it impossible for them to continue to converse with Gracie, she was now starting to think more about what had actually happened to her, about what it might mean by being transferred to Darwin. It was a further distance away from Meeraji Lake, which would no doubt make it difficult for her parents to be with her for any length of time.

'Gracie. Gracie,' she called. 'What words are you going to teach me first?' she asked.

'Uh…umm.' Gracie's breathing was starting to increase and as they started carrying the stretcher towards the helicopter panic filled the teenager's eyes and she started to cry.

'Try and stay calm, Gracie. You've done an amazing job,' Oscar yelled, bending down to speak as close to her ear as he could, but it was difficult when they were all carrying the stretcher, plus having their medical bags on their backs and bending down as they drew ever closer to the whirring chopper blades overhead.

'How long is the flight to Darwin?' Daisy asked Oscar.

'Probably about an hour, maybe a little more,' he yelled.

'And how many bags of fluid do we have?' but her question fell on deaf ears as Oscar continued to watch the teenager, her eyes wide, her breathing becoming more and more erratic.

'Gracie? Gracie, can you hear me?'

She opened her mouth to speak but nothing came out and a moment later she started to shake.

'She's going into shock.' They were almost at the helicopter now, all of them walking more quickly but also being careful they didn't trip over any of the small branches and stringy bark that littered the ground around them.

'Adrenaline is starting to decrease.' Oscar's voice seemed to boom through the area and all of them knew that the sooner they got her into the helicopter, the sooner they'd be able to treat her. It took less than a minute to lift the stretcher into the waiting chopper but it seemed like an eternity to Daisy.

As Tori and Scotty locked the stretcher into place Oscar took his bag off his back and searched through it for the medication he needed. 'She's been so brave for so long,' Daisy stated as she started doing Gracie's observations, while Tori changed over the bag of plasma in order to keep Gracie as hydrated as possible.

'Scotty, wrap the space blanket around her,' Daisy instructed after reporting her observational findings to Oscar. When Tori had finished changing over the plasma bag, Oscar used the IV line to inject some morphine, knowing it would help settle Gracie down even more and keep her calm during transport.

'If you and Oscar take her to Darwin, I'll go back with Scotty and check on Gracie's parents and let them know what's happening,' Tori stated. 'I can organise a flight for them to Darwin so they can be by her side.'

'Thanks.' Daisy pulled off her gloves and put on her headphones, sitting in the seat next to Gracie's, and buckled her seat belt, noting Oscar was doing the same.

'Do you know if anyone has contacted Darwin hospital? And even if they have,' she continued before he had a chance to reply, 'do you think it would be at all possible if I could speak to Timothy before we land? I'd like to give him a fair assessment of what he'll be dealing with.'

Oscar nodded and spoke to the pilot through his headset microphone, asking when it would be possible to get someone from Darwin hospital on the radio.

'We'll be in radio range fairly soon,' came the reply.

'Thank you.' Daisy spoke into her own microphone as she watched Oscar hook a stethoscope into his ears and listen to Gracie's breathing. The teenager's previous agitation seemed to have settled down due to the morphine doing its job. 'It would be good if we could also send Timothy the photos you took.'

'I want to have a better look at them.' Oscar nodded. 'Do you think we'll be able to stay and assist with the surgery? I mean, is this Tim a decent sort or more of a get-out-of-my-theatre type of bloke?'

'Timothy—' she spoke his full name with emphasis '—is most definitely a decent sort of chap and I'm hopeful he'll allow us to at least be present in Theatre. I've assisted with this sort of surgery before and the last one we did took almost twelve hours for the initial surgery. With surgery that long, oftentimes you need to accept all the help you can.'

'We're in range now.' The pilot's voice came through their headphones. 'I'll try and make the connection.' As he did Oscar and Daisy kept monitoring Gracie closely.

'Go ahead, Daisy,' the pilot stated and a moment later Daisy heard Timothy's voice through her headphones.

'Daisy?'

'Timothy.'

'This is getting to be a habit, Dr Forsythe-York,' he stated in his clipped British tones, which seemed to sound perfect alongside Daisy's. 'First you call me about Mrs Piper and show off with your do-gooder generosity and now you no doubt want another favour...or two.'

'Oh, do shut up, Timothy. Listen, I'm bringing a patient to you. A young teenage girl whose right arm got caught in a post-hole digger. Multiple lacerations, dislocated shoulder and olecranon, multiple fractures and extensive tissue damage.'

'Ah. We had been notified of the transfer but I didn't realise you were the treating doctor.'

'One of the doctors,' she added, and continued to explain the situation, giving an update on Gracie's present condition. Oscar added his own opinion to the conversation and let Timothy know he'd taken photographs.

'Is it possible for you to send them to my phone? Daisy should have the number.'

'Still the same one?' she checked.

'Yes.'

'Splendid. We'll get them off to you directly.'

Had her accent become softer as she'd spoken to Timothy? Oscar had to admit that they did sound good together, relaxed, at ease but, then again, they had known each other since medical school so it was only natural they'd speak to each other as old friends because that was exactly what they were.

But were they more than just old friends? It meant nothing to him, of course. He was merely curious…curious about Daisy, about who she really was beneath that sometimes brisk exterior. Never before had a woman intrigued him so much and where that knowledge should have made him cautious, it merely continued to fuel the fire.

Daisy Forsythe-York was an enigma and it was an attribute he found incredibly alluring.

CHAPTER SEVEN

THEY SPENT FAR too many hours in Theatre, watching Timothy and his team perform a miracle. They were even allowed to step in and assist when one of the other doctors became too tired. At one stage, the situation didn't look good and there was a possibility that Gracie might actually need to have her hand amputated, but thankfully that didn't happen. At that moment, Daisy was glad that outback Aussies were as rough as guts and as tough as nails.

'Finally we're out of surgery!' Oscar shuffled out of the theatres, pulling off his cap. 'And that isn't going to be her last operation, poor kid.' Gracie was being wheeled to the intensive recovery unit where she would be closely monitored. 'I haven't done a stint like that since I was an intern.' He smothered a yawn.

'If you don't like it, then never join the armed forces.'

He frowned a little at the tone of her voice. 'I wasn't criticising,' he countered softly and was surprised to see Daisy look instantly contrite.

She closed her eyes for a brief moment before shaking her head. 'I didn't mean it like that.' She hesitated, biting the corner of her lip as she shifted nervously from foot to foot. 'Sometimes, Oscar, when I'm tired…' Daisy paused, forcing herself to say the words even though she already knew what the reaction was going to be. 'It sometimes comes across as being flippant or contradictory or rude. All I meant was that life in the armed forces can be a little...'

'Out of the ordinary?' he supplied and she instantly nodded.

'Yes. Exactly.' She held one hand out to him. 'See? You do understand.' She shook her head as she pulled off her theatre cap and tossed it into the appropriate bin. Then she took out the band and clips that were holding her hair into a loose bun.

Oscar gasped as she raked her fingers through the long locks to try and untangle them. She glanced surreptitiously at him only to find him staring at her in a way that said he most definitely found her attractive. He wasn't leering, he was...looking. And for some reason, she found she liked it. She quickly glanced away, unsure what she was supposed to do when he looked at her in such a way, his eyes saying that he wanted to take his sweet time kissing every inch of her face, to explore the delights she could offer, to savour the flavours of her mouth.

Daisy took a step towards the door. 'I think I'll get changed.' She was shocked to discover her own voice sounding husky and filled with a hint of desire. There was no denying that Oscar Price was an incredibly good-looking man, giving the cliché of tall, dark and handsome some depth of meaning. He was so incredibly different from her past boyfriends that she wondered if that was the reason she was feeling this attraction towards him.

'OK. I'll meet you in the doctors' tearoom and we can decide where we're going to stay tonight.'

Daisy glanced at him again and immediately wished she hadn't. He'd taken a few steps towards the door and was reaching out past her to push it open. She stood, stuck to the spot, unable to move as she looked up at him, his

body close to hers. Lifting her chin, she tried desperately
to make her usually intelligent mind work yet all she was
aware of was his warmth, his subtle spicy scent still evi-
dent even after the long and hot day they'd endured. He
exuded everything that was the epitome of masculinity.
She edged further away, trying desperately to have her
legs compute the signals her brain was sending but all she
felt when she moved were more tingles, more awareness
of just how much Oscar's closeness was affecting her. She
needed to either get out of the room, or throw herself into
his arms. That thought alone helped her to snap her mind
back into gear.

'Well…I shall go and get changed and…er…meet you
in the doctors' tearoom where we can continue with the
conversation about where best to stay this evening.' With
the politest smile she could paste onto her lips, she continued to back out through the open doorway, desperate to
ensure not one part of their bodies touched. When she was
clear, she all but sprinted back towards the female changing rooms, unable to believe everything that had happened
in the past five or so minutes. She caught a glimpse of herself in the mirror and stared in shock. Her cheeks were indeed red, her eyes were dark with a repressed desire and
her lips looked plumper than she'd ever seen before. Her
loose hair was in a wild mess around her face and shoulders, making her look nothing like the poised finishing-
school graduate that she was.

Why had she felt the sudden urge to throw herself into
Oscar's arms? Was it because the other night, when he'd
comforted her, she'd felt as though he'd really cared?
He'd listened to her blubbering, he'd fetched her a drink,
e'd been attentive and kind. He'd supported her and she
hadn't had that kind of support…especially from a man she
found attractive…for a very long time. There was no use

denying to herself that she was attracted to Oscar. She'd lied to herself many years ago, believing her family life was a normal one, and when she'd realised the truth she'd vowed never to lie to herself again. However, although she might accept that she was attracted to Oscar, she also knew there was really nothing she could do about it. At the end of her contract here, she would need to return to the UK, to make one more effort to get her mother into rehab again.

Her mother. Daisy sighed and shook her head. How was she supposed to support her mother effectively from the other side of the world? It was so difficult and gut-wrenching to watch someone you loved waste away from such a disease, especially one that could be helped. She bit her lip and closed her eyes for a split second, remembering how upset she'd been just after speaking to her mother on the phone. Poor Oscar hadn't known what to do and Daisy hadn't known what to say. She *couldn't* tell him. She'd made that mistake years ago with Walter and it had—

No. She wouldn't rehash the past. She'd made a mistake once and she'd learned from it. Talking about her family life was taboo and, besides, she doubted Oscar needed to be bothered by her personal problems. So long as she did her job well, so long as she supported him with the medical needs of the town, then that was all she had to be concerned with. She most certainly didn't need to be distracted by the way he made her feel, by the way he would sometimes stare at her mouth as though he wanted nothing more than just to gather her close and kiss her senseless. Even at the thought, Daisy had to sit down on the bench in the changing rooms because her knees had suddenly decided to give way. Oscar Price was gorgeous. She couldn't deny that and the more she got to know him, the more she liked him as a person.

But they came from very different worlds. His life was

clearly here in Meeraji Lake and her life was… At this moment, she had no idea where her life was. It didn't seem to be in England or working with the army or living in the outback. She was in limbo and she didn't like it one little bit.

Daisy started to feel exhaustion setting in. She'd been running on adrenaline ever since they'd received the call about Gracie, but as she changed out of the theatre scrubs into her own clothes and tidied her hair back into its neat bun again she couldn't seem to stop yawning.

Wherever Oscar was planning to stay, she sincerely hoped it wasn't too far away and when she met him in the doctors' tearoom, she still continued to yawn.

'Good thing we're not planning to head back to Meeraji Lake. You're wrecked,' he said.

'Sorry, I'm…' She yawned. 'I'm trying not to yawn.'

'Go ahead.' He yawned as well and she couldn't help but smile. 'How about we stay across the road in the emergency medical accommodation?'

'We wouldn't be putting other doctors out of a bed, would we? I'm happy to stay at a nearby hotel or something.'

'I'll give the place across the road a call and see what the score is.' Oscar headed to the phone on the wall and dialled the appropriate extension. As he organised their accommodation, she went to the sink and had a glass of water. She was still supposed to be keeping her fluids up after the heatstroke, but after such a gruelling long stint in Theatre it was no wonder she was feeling a little dehydrated.

'All done. Plenty of room with beds to spare for others who may need them. They're also organising for some meals to be sent over.'

'That's very nice.'

'It appears young Gracie is something of a celebrity in medical circles. After all, it isn't every day someone comes in with such an injury and requires extensive surgery to put them back together and, therefore, the doctors who have been looking after her are also entitled to the celebrity treatment.'

'Excellent.' Daisy yawned again and in the next instant realised Oscar was by her side with his arm about her waist.

'Let's get you across the road. You need food and sleep.' They left the doctors' tearoom, Oscar keeping his arm firmly around her waist in case she should collapse. She really was that tired and she was annoyed with herself for feeling so vulnerable when he was around. She needed to keep her guard up, especially when she was this exhausted.

'Could we possibly organise a toothbrush from somewhere, do you think? I can't sleep properly without brushing my teeth.'

'I remember,' he said softly.

'Pardon?'

'That first night when you were delirious from heat exhaustion, you kept asking for your toothbrush.'

'I did?' Embarrassment flooded through her. 'I'm terribly sorry I was such a nuisance.'

'You weren't a nuisance, Daisy. Far from it.'

'Are you laughing at me?' she asked as he led her from the theatre block, calling a few goodbyes to people he knew. Daisy wasn't sure it was a good idea for the two of them to walk through the area with his arm firmly around her waist but at the moment she also wasn't sure whether she could walk unassisted.

'Not at all.'

'Why is it that since I landed in this country, I've been nothing but tired?'

This time he did chuckle. 'Probably because you've been pushing yourself too far, too fast.'

'I always do that. It's my thing.' Her words were barely audible as she yawned twice while speaking.

Daisy wasn't sure of which way they were going but she trusted Oscar to get her where she needed to be. It was odd to be trusting someone she barely knew, but she did. She did trust him. She wasn't sure she'd ever trusted anyone so quickly and she'd had to work in war zones where she'd been reliant upon other people to protect her life. She'd trusted them—in the end—but in the beginning she'd been concerned they wouldn't be able to keep her safe.

Oscar ensured she ate something and then, much to her surprise, he produced a toothbrush and tiny tube of toothpaste from behind his back like a magician. She laughed and gratefully brushed her teeth before slipping between the cool, cotton sheets, the ceiling fan whirring gently overhead.

When Daisy awoke the next morning, she had no idea where she was. She lay still, eyes opened, taking in the surroundings of the room. The whir of the ceiling fan helped her to remember she was in Australia and she relaxed, knowing that it would only take a few weeks before she could wake up and not be alarmed by that feeling of not knowing where she was.

Closing her eyes, she snuggled deeper beneath the sheet, the heat of the day already trying to sneak in behind the closed curtains. It was only then she realised that the light was coming in from a different direction. How was that possible? The curtains in her room were on the left and these curtains were on the right.

She opened her eyes and sat bolt upright in the bed, looking around the room. Then it all came flooding back to her. The emergency with Gracie, staying overnight in Darwin. Oscar! She glanced at the other side of the bed but he wasn't there. She listened carefully. Was he in the en-suite bathroom? She'd been so utterly exhausted the night before, she couldn't remember much of what had happened. Exhaustion had always been her Achilles heel. When she was tired, she became a little delirious. Now, though, she was wide awake and very alert but still couldn't hear any sounds from the bathroom.

Flicking back the sheet, she stood, pleased to see that she was still dressed in the clothes she'd worn beneath her retrieval overalls yesterday. Creeping around to the bathroom, she listened at the closed door for a moment. No sounds. She knocked. No answer. She tentatively opened the door but the room was empty. She quickly made use of the facilities and, when she exited the bathroom, she jumped with surprise at finding Oscar in the room, setting down a tray of food.

'I didn't hear you.' She placed a hand onto her chest in a vain attempt to still her erratic heartbeat. Was it beating so erratically because he'd surprised her? Or because he looked incredibly handsome and refreshed? He, too, was wearing the clothes he'd had on under his retrieval overalls but his hair was slightly damp and his eyes were glowing with a refreshed delight and…and…the man simply looked absolutely gorgeous.

'Is it raining outside?' she asked, knowing that, as Darwin was in the tropics, it would often have torrential rains and still be over thirty degrees Celsius with exceptionally high humidity.

'I had a shower before I went out.'

'Oh. I didn't hear anything. Guess I really was sound asleep.' As she spoke she started to plait her hair, needing to have it out of the way. Oscar wished she wouldn't because she had looked absolutely incredible with it flowing so freely around her shoulders. It had given her a more ethereal look, one of peace, one of contentment.

Last night, she'd woken after sleeping for two or so hours and sat up in bed.

'What's wrong, Daisy?' he'd asked, still a little dozy.

'Hair. Hurts. Need to take it out.' And then her clever fingers had quickly unwound her hair from its usual bun. Her eyes had still been closed and he hadn't been at all sure she was fully awake.

'Are you awake?' he'd asked.

'Of course I'm awake,' she'd replied in that haughty way of hers that he now found so incredibly charming. Daisy had been running her fingers through her now loose strands, tilting her head this way and that, her eyes closed. Good heavens, the woman was beautiful. Had she had no idea of just what she'd been doing to him, sitting there with her perfectly straight back? Tilting her head this way and that and exposing delicious glimpses of her perfect neck? Parting her lips and breathing out a perfect sigh of relief?

With her dark hair spread around her head on the white pillow, she had looked like the perfect vision of loveliness. It had been too much for him. Too much beauty. Too much perfection. Too much... Daisy—the woman who seemed to never be leaving his thoughts. He'd needed to get control. To stop thinking about her in that way. Yes, he was incredibly attracted to her, an attraction that seemed to increase with every passing day he spent in her company, but there could be no future for them. She had her own life to live and he doubted she would want to live it in Meeraji Lake. He wanted the dream, the fairy tale of house, wife, children. Family life. He wanted the typical family life and he felt certain that, for perfect Daisy Forsythe-York, that sort of life would be too mundane.

He'd swallowed, his throat dry. 'Did you want a glass

of water?' Without even waiting for her reply, he'd flicked back the covers and stood, walking to the en-suite.

'What are you wearing?'

He'd turned as the words had seemed to burst forth from her, then glanced down at his boxer shorts. 'My underwear. You might choose to sleep in your clothes but it's not my thing.'

Daisy had frowned at him even more. 'Can't you at least put on a robe?'

'I would, Daisy, if I had one. You're lucky I'm wearing these. I usually sleep naked.' He'd had his drink of water, then returned to the bed. It had been dangerous. Feeling this way about her, lying so close to her, and even though he'd known it was foolhardy, that Daisy would leave Meeraji Lake after her contract was complete, he hadn't been able to stop himself from shifting onto his side and propping himself up on his elbow to look at her.

It was only then he'd realised she'd fallen back into the deep slumber she'd been in before. 'Daisy?' He'd whispered her name. 'Daisy? Are you awake?' His answer had been a small, soft snoring sound and he'd realised that she had indeed been very much asleep.

Lying back down, he'd exhaled a sigh of frustration. She was so close yet so far. Wasn't that the story of his romantic life? Wasn't that what had happened before with both the other women he'd loved? Loved? He didn't love Daisy. He knew that. It was just physical attraction and that was at least something he could control.

'Oscar?'

He blinked once, twice, then pushed aside the memory of last night and focused on her face. 'Sorry? What were you saying?'

She'd finished plaiting her hair and had wound it out of the way into a bun, securing it with another hair band. How it stayed in, he had no idea but all he knew was that she looked so incredibly beautiful first thing in the morning.

'I asked what was for breakfast, seeing as you've clearly gone to the trouble of obtaining it.'

'Uh…yes.' He lifted the warming covers off the food he'd brought in. 'First of all, we have a full English breakfast. Then orange juice, coffee and croissants with jam.'

Daisy peered at the food on the plate. 'Baked beans, scrambled eggs and bacon isn't exactly a full English.' Her stomach chose that moment to gurgle and she grinned. 'But it will definitely suffice.'

Any awkwardness she might have felt from him standing there, staring at her for a good thirty seconds, began to disappear and that comfortable camaraderie they'd established during the other breakfasts and dinners they'd shared seemed to return.

They discussed Gracie and Oscar told her that, while he'd been at the hospital heading to the cafeteria, he'd called by the intensive care unit and checked on the teenager. 'They're keeping her in an induced coma at the moment, in order for her body to recover from the shock of what really happened yesterday.'

'She was so brave. So incredibly stoic about everything.'

'But now reality is looming and she has to face the fact that if she develops complications throughout her recovery period, she may end up losing at least one or two fingers. Timothy, however, is amazing.'

'I know.' Daisy nodded as she took a sip of her coffee. 'He's always been that way. Always knew he wanted to specialise in plastics and to do that minutiae surgery.'

'So why did he go into the army? And what's he doing here in Australia? He could be earning a fortune in the States or in Britain.'

Daisy shrugged. 'Money and prestige aren't that important to him.'

That haughtiness was back in her tone but it was laced with annoyance. What had he said to upset her? 'Are they important to you?'

'No. Most definitely not.'

Well, that was at least something that was different from both Magda and Deidre, he realised.

'You're saying you're not driven by the need to make money?'

'No.' She shook her head and frowned at him. 'Money's not that important.'

'Aha. Only people who have money say that.'

Daisy clenched her jaw and glared at him, then stood from the table, carrying her coffee cup over to the window and most definitely giving him the cold shoulder.

'So you're telling me there's nothing going on between you and Timothy? You've been friends for years, served in the army together and yet there's no romance there?'

'Why does there need to be?' She threw the words over her shoulder. 'Why can't two people simply be colleagues? Why does everyone expect there to be something romantic between us just because we've known each other a long time?'

'Why are you getting so worked up over this?' Oscar eased back in the chair. 'It's a simple question.'

'I haven't heard any question, only supposition and allusion.'

'OK, then. Are you romantically involved with Timothy?'

'Why do you need to know?'

'Come on, Daisy. I just asked you a straight-out question and you're still not going to answer it?' When she didn't immediately respond, still standing there at the window with her back to him, he couldn't help but prod a little further. 'It's not such an unusual question—after all, you did come to Australia around the same time he did.'

'That was completely coincidental.' She drank the rest of her coffee and turned to glare at him. 'I don't see what any of this has to do with you.'

'It's just seeing the two of you together, seeing how you work well with each other, having your own shorthand to convey what it is you need the other to do—'

'We worked together in very difficult circumstances in a very unsafe environment. Developing the shorthand was necessary and came out of constant experience. And besides, he is one of my closest friends. Probably my oldest friend, if truth be told, and I actually don't have that many friends.'

'You don't?'

'No.' She walked towards the table and started clearing up their breakfast dishes.

'Do you want to talk about it?'

'No.'

'Does it have anything to do with the way you were crying the other night?'

'What? No.'

'Well, it's difficult to get a read on you, Daisy. You're so incredibly closed off. You keep yourself to yourself and, while that's generally fine in a large medical setting, at Meeraji Lake it's impossible to keep your distance from others without feeling ostracised by the township.'

'I understand that and I have actually been opening myself up to others.'

He shook his head at this. 'You've been receptive to others telling you things about themselves but you most certainly don't open yourself up to others. I've asked you a simple question and yet you've gone and blown it all out of proportion.'

'No. You were fishing. Wanting to know if there was anything romantic going on between me and Timothy because you have feelings for me.'

He raised an eyebrow at that.

'Oh, don't deny it. I've seen the way you look at me.'

'And I've seen the way you look at me,' he countered. 'So is there anything, other than friendship, going on between you and Timothy?'

'Why?' She spread her arms wide. 'Why is it so important for me to tell you the most intimate details of my life when I'll be gone in less than six months?'

'Why indeed?' he growled and, without another word, picked up the tray of dirty dishes and headed for the door.

'Where are you going?' she asked, but received no reply except for the room door closing behind him.

CHAPTER EIGHT

DAISY PACED AROUND the room, fuming with annoyance and swamped with regret. It wasn't fair to Oscar that she'd exasperated him by not providing him with the answers he wanted but, at the end of the day, it really wasn't any of his business whether or not she was involved with Timothy or anyone else for that matter.

Except that perhaps he'd been trying to ask her whether she was single, whether she was available for a…for a what? For a relationship that lasted for the duration of her contract? What sort of relationship did he want? She had to admit that the thought of getting closer to Oscar wasn't entirely unpalatable but what would be the point? She needed to return to the UK, to check on her mother, to do whatever it was that needed to be done to ensure that Cecilia didn't end up drinking herself into an early grave. Starting something with Oscar, especially when she knew it wouldn't end well due to the fact that they lived on opposite sides of the globe and wanted different things from life, would be ludicrous.

At least she thought they wanted different things from life. She hadn't really asked Oscar what he wanted but she was sure that, as he seemed to be a strong family-man sort of chap, a man who counted every person in the town and the surrounding district of Meeraji Lake as his family, he would most definitely want a family of his own. Was that the reason why he'd been married once and engaged the next time? His only problem, as far as she knew, was that he'd chosen the wrong women.

Daisy sat down at the table where they'd eaten their breakfast and slumped forward. It was such an unladylike pose and one she'd been told off for many times during her younger years at home. Even though she was thirty-eight years old, she could still hear her mother's admonishing voice, telling her to sit up straight, shoulders back. That was the way a lady sat. Daisy still hated the fact that the rules her parents had drummed into her seemed to resonate at the most inopportune moments.

When the door to the room opened, Daisy immediately sat up straight, her finishing-school training kicking in.

'Still here, eh?' Oscar walked into the room and headed to the bathroom to wash his hands.

'Where else was I supposed to go? I've already spoken to the hospital and received an update on Gracie. I don't know the city, I don't know where the airport is and I don't know how we're supposed to get back to Meeraji Lake.'

He came out of the bathroom, hand towel in his hands as he thoroughly dried them. 'I apologise, Daisy. I shouldn't have walked out on you. It's just that sometimes—' He threw the towel onto the bed and crossed his arms over his chest. 'Sometimes you drive me crazy.'

'The feeling is mutual.' She stood and faced him, mimicking his stance and crossing her arms over her chest. 'But…' She relaxed for a moment, dropping her hands to her side. 'You weren't totally blameless for what happened. I'm sorry, too. I didn't mean to rile you up.'

'It's just sometimes that—' he held out a hand towards her '—Britishness of yours really grates on my nerves.'

'And that Aussieness of yours does the same to mine. I

don't have to tell you about every aspect of my life, Oscar. The residents of Meeraji Lake may like everyone knowing their business but I'm British. We don't talk about our feelings even when we want to.' She spread her arms wide. 'I've been raised to repress that natural urge to share, to discuss. I was told it wasn't ladylike to prattle on about one's problems or the mundane nuances of my life. I was warned that no one would be interested.'

'I'm interested.' He raked his hands through his hair. 'I *want* to know all about the mundane nuances of your life. I want to know if you have a boyfriend, a fiancé, a husband. I want to know what your favourite foods are, what colours you like, what plans you have for your future. I'm interested, Daisy.'

'Because you like me?'

'Yes!' He laughed with exasperation, then shook his head.

'Timothy is not my boyfriend. Not now, nor in the past and never in the future.'

'You can't be sure of that.'

'Oh, I can. You see, he's gay.'

Oscar stared at her for a moment, then blinked one long blink. 'I didn't…er…realise.'

'Not many people do. He likes to keep it quiet. He hasn't "come out" as they say nowadays. He's a respected surgeon, a brilliant surgeon and, believe it or not, his personal preferences can and will affect his career if it becomes common knowledge.'

'I won't say a word.'

'Thank you.'

'And thank you.' When she raised her eyebrows in question, he added, 'For trusting me.'

She smiled at him then and began to relax a little, sit-

ting down at the table. 'What's happening with our transport back to Meeraji Lake?'

'I'm waiting on the Royal Flying Doctor Service to call
me. They'll be able to take us back, it's just a question of
when. In the meantime,' he said, going to the cupboard
and taking out the teacups and electric kettle, 'why don't
we have another cuppa and you can tell me some of your
tales about your time in the army?' He looked thoughtful for a moment. 'I've thought about joining the army.'

'You?' She couldn't help the laughter that bubbled up
with the word.

'Why? What's wrong with me going into the Army?'

'Uh…lack of discipline for a start. You'd have to be the
class clown, wouldn't you?'

'What's wrong with enjoying a laugh every now and
then?'

'Having a laugh, as you call it, might jolly well get your
head blown off.' Oscar laughed at her words and she shook
her head. 'You're pulling my leg, aren't you?'

'Yes.' He pointed to the cups. 'Tea?'

She nodded and while she watched him make them
both a drink she talked with enthusiasm about her work
in the army.

'How isolated were you?' he questioned.

'Most of the time, we were in compounds. We worked
alongside a lot of Americans as well as Australians and
New Zealanders. It wasn't safe. It wasn't pretty. It was difficult operating in a tent, especially when patients were in
such life-threatening situations. One time, there were big
trucks rumbling past not too far away from where Timothy
and I were trying to operate, removing bullet fragments
from a soldier's chest.'

'It must have been frightening.'

'Working with Timothy?' She wilfully misunderstood.

He smiled, pleased to see her sense of humour was definitely intact. 'Yes.'

'It was terrifying,' she replied, her smile big and bright and absolutely beautiful. Oscar tried not to sigh from just staring into her eyes. The more time he spent with her, the more he was liking her...wanting to kiss her...wanting to hold her close and never let her— He stopped his thoughts before his mind could finish that sentence.

'Why did you go? What made you sign up for duty?' The moment he spoke, he saw her jaw clench and she glared at him.

'Do I need a reason?'

'Don't give me that look,' he retorted with light humour, shaking his finger at her. 'It's a fair question. The army doesn't suit everyone, as you've so aptly pointed out.' He indicated himself as he spoke.

'True. I think I needed to prove something.'

'To yourself? Or someone else?'

She thought for a moment. 'Perhaps it was a bit of both.'

'Your...father?' Her quick look told him he was correct. 'Did your father want you to go into the army to toughen you up or didn't he think you could handle it?'

'The latter but now I have to wonder if he didn't goad me into it.' She closed her eyes and shook her head slightly. 'When I'm not staying with them at the big house, he has full control over my mother. Then again, maybe I felt guilty after what I'd done.' She opened her eyes and shrugged. 'I guess we'll never know.' She was still sitting quietly, clearly lost in contemplation.

'Would you like to talk about it?' he asked, hoping against hope that she would.

'Talk about what? My father? My mother? My life in the army?'

'Whatever it is you want to tell me. I'm interested in *all* aspects of your life,' he stated and she looked at him with surprise. The fact that Oscar was interested in her, that he wanted to know more about her, was willing to listen to what she had to say, was such a nice thing that she found herself wanting to tell him.

She bit her lip, then stood and walked over to the window, looking out through the lace curtains at the bustling city outside. So much was going on, cars speeding up and slowing down, traffic lights changing, seagulls squawking. She watched them all unseeingly as she spoke, her quiet tone quiet.

'If you think I talk all posh, then you'll find my parents almost over the top.' She was trying to inject a bit of humour into her words and he wondered whether that was because she was nervous at opening up to him. 'My father rules the roost, controlling everyone and everything that happens in his house.'

'What about your brother? Does he live close to your parents?'

'John? Yes, he and his family live on the estate.'

'You have an estate?'

She shook her head and looked at him. 'My *father* has an estate. *John* has an estate. John's *son* has an estate. It's inherited through the first-born male. My father is most definitely stuck in the past, not moving with the times and intent on upholding tradition.'

'Tradition is clearly important to him.'

'It's how he was raised. At any rate, he was pleasantly surprised with my grades from medical school and seemed quite pleased his daughter was a doctor. It was an accomplishment.'

'That's a good thing.'

'You'd think that.' Daisy pursed her lips. 'Once I'd completed my training and was qualified, he decided I should go into practice with an old friend of his who had been our family doctor since…well, since before I was born.'

'That wasn't what you wanted?'

She spread her arms wide. 'No, but did that matter to my father? Not in the slightest. I was to do as I was told.'

'How old were you? Mid-twenties?'

'Yes, but as far as my father's concerned I'm a woman and so I couldn't possibly make up my own mind or know what's good for me. He's a dictatorial control freak and I—' She stopped and closed her eyes, forcing herself to take some calming breaths. 'My mother encouraged me to leave home, to try working overseas.'

'She was on your side?'

Daisy looked at him and nodded. 'She didn't want me to end up living the same life she'd been forced into. Of course, after I left, my father blamed her for corrupting me.'

'He doesn't sound like a very nice man.' Oscar held up his hands in apology. 'Sorry. I know I don't even know him, but—'

'You're right, though. He isn't nice. He's manipulative and exceedingly arrogant. If he can't control your life, he'll make it a living hell.'

'But you've escaped?'

'To a point. My mother isn't…um…in the best of health.' She was choosing her words carefully and he received the distinct impression that there was more to the situation, especially where her mother's health was concerned, than she was letting on. 'Because of that I have to keep going home to help her.'

Oscar reflected on the conversation he'd overheard. 'And your brother? Does he help your mother?'

'More out of duty, rather than because he's concerned

about her.' She laughed without humour. 'Both he and my father always say I'm overreacting.'

'But as a medical professional, you clearly have knowledge that they don't.'

'Exactly. Thank you. I'm not overreacting and my mother's condition…I've tried to get her help and she'll accept it, to a point but then—' Daisy stopped and sighed as though she was exhausted from even thinking about it. She crossed to the bed and sat down, relaxing a little. 'If I stay too long at home, my mother often tells me to leave. In the nicest way, of course. Besides, I can only take so much of my father and his autocratic behaviour.'

'So you ran away and joined the army?'

She grinned. 'I didn't exactly run away. Timothy was already in the army reserves but then when they were calling for full-time medical doctors to head into the combat zone, I figured that if I could handle my father, I could handle anything.'

'Stubborn?'

Her smile increased and she nodded. 'I am.'

'I know.'

'Hey!'

'Have you already forgotten that you were ill when you first arrived? You were stubborn to the point of annoyance.'

'*I* was annoying? Ha. I think it was the other way around,' she told him, her eyes twinkling with mirth as she pointed her finger at him. He moved to sit beside her on the bed and grabbed her finger.

'Point that thing back at you.'

She laughed, a sound he could most definitely become addicted to…if he wasn't already. 'I think we should agree to disagree on this point.'

'Or agree that we're both as stubborn as each other,'

he added, lacing his fingers with hers. The action caused her to tremble a little and she quickly looked into his eyes, nervousness mixed with excitement bubbling through her. They were sitting so close, his hypnotic scent filling her senses and causing butterflies to churn in her stomach.

He was sitting so close. Smelling so good. Driving her crazy. They shouldn't be looking at each other like this. They were colleagues. They were…friends? She certainly didn't tell just anyone about her family. Oscar was someone she'd come to trust but she'd made the mistake of trusting the wrong person before and she couldn't make it again. She swallowed as she continued to stare at him. How was it that he could set her insides on fire by just looking at her, by visually caressing her face? How was it that she wanted him to kiss her, to press sweet and tender kisses on her cheeks, her eyelids, her forehead? She couldn't remember the last time she'd been so attracted to a man, as quickly as she'd become attracted to Oscar.

She swallowed again, her lips parting to allow the pent-up air to escape. She glanced at the clock beside the bed and cleared her throat, trying to deny the senses he was awakening. 'We…uh…should probably head over to the hospital.'

'Daisy.' Her name was a caress upon his lips and some-how he'd shifted even closer to her, or perhaps she was only now realising how easy it would be to lean over and press her mouth to his. Her breath hitched when he put his other hand beneath her chin, smoothing his thumb over her parted lips.

'Daisy.' How could he say her name in such a way that caused desire to rip through her, desire for him to want her, need her, kiss her? She wanted Oscar to kiss her. She'd dreamed about it and now the moment was here, the moment when she could find out how this wonderful man could make her feel. Instinctively she knew it was going to be good. It just had to be. Oscar was handsome and intelligent and delightful to spend time with.

She closed her eyes, feeing his light breath fan in her face. He was going to kiss her. Oscar wanted to kiss her! Her lips opened a little further in anticipation, her heart pounding wildly against her chest, her senses on alert as she waited...waited...

His lips brushed hers in an exceedingly light but delicious way and she all but melted towards him. 'Mmm...' Had that sound come from her or him? He didn't try to deepen the kiss, didn't try to rush, instead he seemed more than content to brush another small kiss across her lips, their breaths mingling and dissolving together.

His hand at her chin slowly shifted around to rest just below her ear, cupping her cheek while his other hand tightened around hers, the actions showing her his restraint at not allowing himself to get carried away. It was as though he wanted to treasure her, wanted to let her know that this wasn't something he did every day, that she was special.

Whether or not Daisy was reading too much into the way he was treating her, she had no idea, but just as he eased back, opening his mouth to hopefully deepen the kiss, to give them both what they appeared to want, his cell phone rang, piercing the air around them. Daisy instantly jumped with fright at the sound and pulled away from him.

Oscar growled and removed his phone from his pocket, turning his back to her as he answered the call, saying a few clipped words here and there before hanging up. He tossed his phone onto the table and shoved both hands into his pockets. He looked her way but didn't hold her gaze. What did that mean? Did he regret what had happened between them?

'That was the Royal Flying Doctor Service. They have a plane heading to Meeraji Lake in thirty minutes with room for two passengers.'

'That's good news.' Daisy needed to do something, needed to be busy, to find a way to distract her thoughts. She stood and started pulling the coverings off the bed they'd shared.

'What are you doing?'

'What does it look like I'm doing?' Her words came out in that haughty way of hers even though she didn't mean them in such a fashion. 'I'm removing the sheets from the bed.'

'But they have cleaners. They can do it,' he stated, looking at her as though she was a little crazy.

'And just think how that person is going to feel when they walk into this room and see one less job they have to do. It might just make their day and if that's the case, then I'm happy to do it.'

'Huh.' Oscar nodded. 'I hadn't thought about it that way before,' he said and immediately picked up a pillow and removed the pillow case.

The truth of the matter was that being near him, having kissed him so tantalisingly, had made her more nervous than a long-tailed cat in a room full of rocking chairs. Daisy had needed to do something to expel the nervous energy zipping through her and doing something practical had been the solution.

'Where do we need to meet the plane?' she asked, picking up the edge of the blanket and starting to fold it. Oscar immediately grabbed the other end and helped her.

'We need to take a taxi to the airport and head to the RFDS airstrip.'

'And we only have half an hour to do that?' She folded the blanket with him, then automatically walked towards him to grasp the two ends together. It was a mistake. Their fingers touched and her body pulsed with a longing and need she'd had no idea she possessed. Her heart rate increased as they stood there, close once more with a neatly folded blanket between them. Daisy hugged the blanket to her as she watched him swallow, before meeting his gaze.

'It will only take about ten minutes to get there.' His voice was soft, deep, intimate, just as it had been before when they'd kissed. Daisy closed her eyes, unable to really understand what was happening to her. Why did he have to smell so good? Why did the pheromones exuding from both of them mingle perfectly together to make one highly potent concoction?

'Ordinarily I can control my emotions.' Her words were as soft as a whisper but she knew he could hear her. Their senses were overly attuned to each other, heightened, sensitised. 'I was raised to quash all emotions and, between medical school and the army, I've learned to compartmentalise everything.'

'Including what you want? What you need?'

Daisy opened her eyes and looked at him. 'Yes. Honour and duty come first. To the monarchy. To family. To the armed forces.'

'You're not in the UK now. Your family is not here either and you're no longer in the army.' Oscar reached out and brushed his fingers across her cheek before lifting her chin a little higher. Then, before she could say or do anything else, he lowered his head and brushed his lips across hers, this time with a little more pressure. It was as though he intended there to be absolutely no doubt that he wanted to kiss her, that he wanted to be near her, that he was attracted to her.

Daisy started to shake, her breathing coming so fast she thought she might hyperventilate. Thankfully, Oscar made no further effort to deepen the contact between them, seemingly content to repeat the gentle, sensual action again and again. It was as though he was trying to memorise every contour, every nuance, every flavour she provided.

Never before had any man treated her in such a way that made her feel precious and treasured and appreciated. That was what he was doing. He was appreciating her mouth, appreciating *her*.

Daisy stepped back, her heart pounding wildly against her chest, her blood thrumming through her body so much, the sound was reverberating in her ears. She dropped the blanket but didn't bother to bend down and pick it up. Instead, she stared at Oscar as though he was something too good to be true. It was always the way.

In the past, when she'd been interested in a man, nine times out of ten he'd been more interested in her family money, or the prestige her family name might provide. However, if what she was feeling for Oscar, especially having only known him for such a short time, was this powerful, hungry desire, then something had seriously been lacking in her life. The question now remained, what did it all mean? What did it mean to him? Did he want money? Did he really find her attractive? What were his motives?

Licking her dry lips, Daisy took a few deep breaths, trying to get her wayward breathing to settle into a more even rhythm. 'We'd...' She cleared her throat when her voice cracked. 'We'd best get to the plane.'

With that, she bent to pick up the blanket and continued to tidy the room. Oscar just stood there, watching her as though he really didn't understand what was going on. When she was done, she walked to the door, not waiting for him. There was a taxi rank across the road outside the front of the hospital and, leaving him to gather his personal items and lock the door behind them, she continued across the road to flag down their transport.

When he joined her in the taxi, sitting in the back seat while she sat in the front with the driver, Oscar seemed his usual jovial self, chatting and laughing with the driver as though they were old friends instead of two people who had just met.

At the airport, he was the same with the RFDS staff, although, she discovered, he really was old friends with most of them. He introduced Daisy to everyone, ensured her seat belt was correctly fastened before take-off and showed her every courtesy as though nothing weird, crazy or sensual had happened between them.

All it did was confuse her even more.

CHAPTER NINE

WHEN THEY RETURNED from Darwin, Oscar continued to be his usual polite self towards Daisy. He behaved this way because he had no idea what he was meant to do after kissing her. Should he kiss her again? Hold her hand in the taxi? Whisper in her ear during the plane ride back to Meeraji Lake?

He'd been so unnerved by the way she'd responded to him, by the way she had smelled so sweet and delicious. Why had he kissed her? When he'd taken the breakfast tray back to the hospital cafeteria, he'd been so incredibly annoyed with her, wondering why she hadn't been able to trust him, to open up and then…when she had, it had stirred all his protective instincts.

It was then he'd realised that her reticence, her reluctance to discuss her life with him, was more attributed to her repressed upbringing than not wanting to confide in him. He also couldn't deny he'd been pleased to hear that she wasn't Timothy's type and, while he had nothing against the brilliant surgeon, it had been a relief to know that Daisy wasn't attached to him. None of this, however, explained why Oscar had finally given in to the urges he'd been fighting so successfully up to that point and kissed her!

Because he hadn't been able to stop himself. The

woman had managed to get under his skin, to become a part of his dreams and after lying next to her all night long, and with their heightened emotions, when the moment had arisen he'd grabbed it with both hands. The only problem with his actions was now that he knew how wonderful she felt in his arms, now that he knew how perfectly her lips seemed to meld to his own, now that he'd tasted the delicious flavours of her mouth, he most definitely wanted more. Much more. And that was indeed a major problem.

Daisy would leave at the end of her contract and now he knew why. Looking after and supporting her mother was a noble cause. He could also understand why she'd previously said that she never wanted to have a family herself, because her own family life hadn't been a happy one. His upbringing, although filled with sadness when his parents had passed away, had still been a happy one. He'd been encouraged, he'd been supported and he'd been loved.

From what Daisy had said, she'd had very little of any of those things, and it pained him to think of what she might have been through in the past. All of this, however, meant that kissing her had been the absolute wrong thing to do. He knew he wanted to stay here in Meeraji Lake, to get married and raise a family. Yes, he was concerned about getting involved with a woman again, opening his heart up once more and risking it being broken, and with Daisy he was almost ninety-nine per cent sure that would happen. If he continued down his present path, of wanting to spend more time with her, of wanting to talk more about her past, of learning everything there was to know about Daisy Forsythe-York, then he would definitely end up with another broken heart.

Surely it would be best for both of them if they forgot all about those kisses and went back to just being colleagues. Wouldn't it?

* * *

A week later, Daisy still had no idea what was really going on in Oscar's head, not where the attraction between the two of them was concerned. When they'd returned to Meeraji Lake, Oscar had been his usual kind and considerate self. He'd made her breakfast every morning for the next week, had helped her cook dinner in the evenings and had brought her a cup of tea just before she'd headed to bed. They would often sit and chat about movies they both liked as well as discussing different books, offering recommendations or lending each other the title.

When he said goodnight to her, he would politely kiss her hand then bid her sweet dreams before disappearing down to his end of the house. He'd made no reference to the kisses they'd shared nor had he made any other effort to drag her close and plunder her mouth once more…even though she'd continually dreamed he would.

It was as though those kisses had never happened and she could only conclude that he now regretted the impulse and wanted to forget about it. She tried not to let that knowledge bother her, tried not to take it personally, to compartmentalise her feelings, but at the end of it all he was making it quite clear he only wanted a professional relationship with her. Well, if that was the case, she could be just as nonchalant about it, just as dismissive of it and just as kind and polite to him as he was to her.

So why did he still kiss her hand every night and look at her with eyes that were filled with repressed desire and bid her sweet dreams?

'What's going on between you and Oscar?' Tori asked her one day after clinic had finished. Daisy had walked into the hospital to find it almost eerily quiet so had sat down to catch up on some of the paperwork.

'You tell me and we'll both know,' she stated with a sigh.

'Do you *want* something to happen between the two of you?' Tori persisted.

Daisy put her pen down and looked at the nurse with confusion. 'I don't know. I'm only here for a six-month contract and then I'll be leaving. Is it really worth starting anything up with him?'

'Fair point. That's what happened between him and Deidre. He thought she'd stay permanently, in fact we all did, but then, when her contract was up, she decided to leave instead. She was more than happy for him to come with her but she wasn't going to stay in the outback for any longer than she had to.' Tori shook her head. 'She had us all fooled.'

'She'd given him no indication she was going to leave?'

'None whatsoever. They were engaged and she was talking about their wedding here and starting a family and then—' She shrugged. 'I don't know. Something just happened and she left.'

'And you don't know what it was?' Daisy asked.

'I do,' a deep male voice said from behind them and they both turned to see Oscar standing near the door to the ED. Daisy was instantly embarrassed and quickly looked away, annoyed with herself for gossiping about him. Tori took one look at the scowl on his face and made herself scarce. 'It's all right, Oscar. You don't need to tell me.' Daisy cleared her throat. 'Tori mentioned Deidre.'

'It's OK. I don't mind. The truth was that Deidre received a better offer.' Oscar walked over and pulled up a chair, sitting next to Daisy. 'Because of her outback medicine training and experience, she was head-hunted—at least that's what she told me, but I have a feeling she'd applied for the job—for the position of consultant to the minister of health, particularly concerning the health of native Australians. Three times the pay she was getting here and a lot more prestige.'

'That must have been incredibly difficult for you, Oscar,' Daisy stated.

He nodded. 'She even offered to give me the engagement ring back but I didn't want it. I didn't have time to grieve over the breakdown of the relationship as Lucinda was really ill by then and needed all my attention.'

'And being the true hero that you are, you gave her everything she needed.'

'Just as she gave me everything I needed when our parents passed away.'

'You're fortunate to have had that one special person in your life.'

'True. She was a great sister and I still miss her.'

'Of course you do.' Daisy's heart was breaking for him and, without thinking, she reached over and took his hand in hers. 'I'm so sorry for what you've been through.'

He met her gaze, hopefully realising she was genuine in her words. 'I'm becoming quite adept at recovering from being abandoned.' He tried to inject humour into his words but ended up sighing with a heaviness of heart. 'First my wife, Magda, decided she didn't want to be with me any more and left me for another man, someone who could give her more money than I ever could. Then I move here and Deidre breaks my heart and then my sister dies.'

'You really have been through the wringer.'

'Well, from what you've said, your life hasn't exactly been a picnic.'

She grimaced and nodded. 'We all have our crosses to bear.'

He gave Daisy's hand a little squeeze then let it go, standing up and walking to the other side of the desk.

Was he trying to put distance between them? To keep her questions at bay?

'If you don't want to talk about it, Oscar, I completely understand.'

'It's all right, Daisy. I probably owe you some sort of explanation.'

'For what?'

'For kissing you and then keeping you at arm's length.'

'It's all right—' she started to say, but stopped. She did want to know what he was thinking and as he was offering to talk to her, she'd be stupid to refuse him. 'Actually, tell me whatever you feel comfortable telling me.'

He smiled then, causing a mass of tingles to flood through her at the sight. 'OK.' He still kept his distance, standing on the other side of the desk, arms crossed over his chest. It seemed to take a while for him to gather his thoughts but eventually he spoke. 'Kissing you...I shouldn't have done it.'

Daisy bit her lip, mainly to keep it from wobbling and to hold the threatening tears at bay. It was one thing to think it, to come to that conclusion on her own, but to have him come right out and say that he regretted kissing her—

'That doesn't mean I didn't enjoy it,' he added quickly and she wondered whether she'd been adept at controlling her expression or whether he now knew her well enough to read her face accurately. 'I did. Oh, I did.'

'I did, too.' Her words were a whisper.

'But it can't be, Daisy. Surely you see that.'

'I'm leaving at the end of my contract.'

'Yes.'

'I *have* to go back to England and check on my mother, try again at another attempt to get her to leave my father but...but she loves him and takes all his—' She stopped, realising every muscle in her body was tense. She forced herself to relax. 'But that's not what we're discussing.'

'I admire you for caring for your mother, for being so concerned about her that you effectively put your own life on hold until you can be sure she's OK. That's what family is all about. Being there for each other.'

'Yes. I guess it is. My brother sees it merely as doing his duty.'

'And that's where you're different from him—you care, genuinely care for your mother and her well-being. That's, as I said, admirable and therefore I can't even get mad at you for leaving.'

'Were you hoping to talk me into staying longer?'

'That was my initial plan when I advertised the position.'

'Why not advertise it for twelve months, then?'

'Well…partly because it's difficult to get doctors out here at the best of times and offering only a six-month contract provides more chance of success at filling the vacancy.'

'And the other part of the reason?'

'Because of Deidre. She was here for twelve months, she told me she felt locked into it and although she had planned on staying, said she liked it here, when that other job offer came up, it was only then she remembered what her life had been like before she'd come to Meeraji Lake. Does that make any sense?'

'Yes.' She smiled. 'I can see how being here feels as though you're in another world. I love it.'

'And, in the end, Deidre didn't.'

'So what will you do when I leave? Advertise for another six-month position?'

'More than likely.'

She thought on this for a moment. 'Did your wife—?'

'Magda.'

'Did Magda ever come to Meeraji Lake?'

'Magda?' He laughed without humour. 'No. No, this wasn't the place for her.'

'What was she like? Er...do you mind me asking?'

'No.' He raked a hand through his hair with frustration. 'Magda was...duplicitous. That's probably the best word to describe her.' He shook his head. 'I was so blind. She was beautiful and funny to work with. I was living in Brisbane, that's in Queensland,' he added and she nodded, indicating she knew where Brisbane was. 'Anyway, Magda was a nurse on the ward where I was working and she was absolutely lovely.' He re-crossed his arms over his chest. 'In hindsight, I've realised she was more of a chameleon, changing the way she was in order to get what she wanted.'

'And she wanted you?'

'She wanted a doctor who had prospects, who could keep her in the lifestyle she'd always wanted. One time, she even confessed to me that she'd only completed her nursing training because she knew it was the best way to secure a rich doctor as a husband. It wasn't until after our honeymoon that she began to change. First, she decided to go part-time at work and then she quit altogether.'

'That didn't bother you?'

He looked past Daisy, as though he was looking back into his past, his tone filled with regret. 'She told me she had a better chance of falling pregnant if she wasn't so stressed because of work.'

'She didn't get pregnant?' Daisy surmised.

'She was taking birth-control pills the entire three years of our marriage.' He sighed. 'Her expenses started to increase, she'd go shopping, have lunch with a lot of the other surgeons' wives. It was an exclusive club to her and because she was married to me, she'd gained access.

'Then she encouraged me to apply for a job in Sydney and I was successful. It was longer hours but more money.'

'What she wanted?'

'All along. We bought an enormous house, far bigger than we needed, but it had a pool and a tennis court and was good for entertaining and holding networking parties...which she did.'

Daisy nodded, thinking of her father's estate, which was more than three times the size of what Oscar was describing. 'Were you happy?'

'I thought I was. I did meet a lot of influential people, which helped me to secure more money for my research projects.'

'Not what you know but who you know?'

'Exactly, but it reached the point where I was working long hours all week at the hospital, working at home, sleeping less, stressing more and then having to be the host at one of Magda's networking parties on the weekends. It was all just too much and when I asked her to stop—at least for a while—she exploded.'

'Not literally, I hope.' Daisy grinned and was thankful when Oscar returned her smile, and the tension that had tightened his shoulders as he'd spoken of his ex-wife visibly started to decrease. 'So things just sort of fizzled out between the two of you?'

'Sort of. Lucinda was diagnosed with breast cancer and, although she had a double mastectomy, the chemotherapy would only hold it at bay for a while. I instantly resigned from my job and made arrangements to move here to Meeraji Lake.'

'Magda wasn't too thrilled?'

'If I thought she'd exploded before, it was nothing compared to how she reacted to that news. It was then she told me that she'd been taking birth-control pills throughout our entire three-year marriage, that she'd had several affairs with other men and that as far as a husband who could provide reasonably for his wife was concerned, I was a failure and she was moving on.'

'She filed for divorce?'

'Yes.'

'And you moved to Meeraji Lake?'

'Yes.'

She pondered his words for a moment before saying softly, 'Life's a strange thing, sometimes. The connections we make can either bring us joy or disaster.'

'Have you had many relationship disasters?'

'There are always bad relationships in everyone's history,' she stated and he could see her clamming up.

'Not quite ready to talk about it?'

'Is anyone ever ready to talk about their failures?'

'I just did.'

'Why? Why did you?'

Oscar came and sat back down next to her. 'Because maybe I'm crazy. Maybe I'm making a mistake, opening up to you instead of pushing you away.' He reached for her hand. 'I've been trying so hard to fight it, Daisy, but when it comes down to the bottom line, I'm attracted to you.'

'And you don't want to be.' She nodded and slowly pulled her hand back. Oscar looked up at the ceiling and exhaled harshly.

'I don't know, Daisy. You make me feel like I haven't felt in a long time. You make me believe in a future when for quite some time I was more than content just to go from day to day. So much has happened to me, two women I've loved have let me down. My parents and my sister passed away. I don't know if I'm the sort of man who needs to be married, who needs the stability of a wife beside him and, if I am, perhaps that comes from being orphaned at such a young age.'

He looked deeply into her eyes. 'All I know is that when I'm around you, I'm happy.'

'Being happy is good.' She nodded and found that for a long moment she simply couldn't look away. What was it about him that she found so compelling, so exciting, so hypnotic? She agreed with everything he was saying and yet she knew deep down inside that there couldn't possibly be a happily ever after for the two of them together. They lived on opposite sides of the world; they had different priorities in their lives. Daisy had vowed that, after her previous disastrous relationship, she wasn't going to venture back into that ring for quite some time. She was going to focus on her career; she was going to look after her mother and hopefully start a new life for the two of them somewhere away from her father.

'Right?' His gaze dropped to her lips and she felt her heart rate instantly increase. 'So when you find someone who makes you happy, why should it be the right thing to pull away from them?'

Daisy couldn't help but lick her parted lips, watching him watch her. The tension between them was so real and as vital as breathing and yet it was a hopeless situation. 'Because there's no hope for a future together.' Her words were barely above a whisper but she knew he'd heard them as he closed his eyes, almost as though he was trying to block out the vision of her sitting there before him.

'Daisy.' He breathed her name. 'Those kisses…'

'Oscar, don't.'

He looked at her. 'Denying the way you make me feel is making me ill. I'm not sleeping properly, I'm only eating well because we eat two meals a day together and I really like spending that time with you, getting to know you a bit better even when I know I should be putting more distance between us.'

'We have to work together, live in the same house together. To have that fraught with tension—'

'It's already fraught with tension.'

'Negative tension,' she clarified. 'To live like that would be unbearable for the duration of my contract. I don't want that.'

'Neither do I, which is why a professional and light friendship seems the best way to go and yet when you laugh, or unplait your hair and—' He stared at her mouth once more and sighed with longing.

'Should I move out?'

'No.' The word was instant.'

'Do you think we ought to…?'

'What?' he prompted when she stopped.

Daisy dragged in a deep breath then blurted out what she was thinking. 'Do you think we ought to discuss those…' she cleared her throat '…those kisses we shared?'

'I've thought about that.' He moved his chair a little closer to hers and reached out to take her hand in his, entwining their fingers just as he had before the last time he'd kissed her. 'I just didn't think it was a good idea to discuss it at our house.'

Our house? Even those words caused her heart rate to flutter. 'Why not? We're alone there and less likely to be interrupted.'

'That's why. Because we're *alone* there and I'm not sure talking about kissing you is sensible when I'm then able to kiss you and hold you close and then…' His voice had become thick and husky with repressed desire as he'd spoken the quiet words and her eyes half closed, as though she was quite capable of imagining the perfect conclusion those kisses might reach. 'Daisy.' Her name was a caress upon his lips. 'I can't ignore any more the way you make me feel.'

'Feel?' The word was so soft she wasn't even sure she'd spoken it out loud.

'Yes.' He shifted closer, bringing his chair right up against hers. Daisy was too stunned, too overpowered by her wayward emotions, by the heated tingles that ran from her fingers, up her arm to explode throughout her entire body. Her breathing had increased, her mouth had gone dry and even her knees were weakening at his touch. Why was it that she turned into a hormonal teenager at one simple look from him, or one gentle touch, or one absolutely incredibly sensual kiss?

'We do need to talk about it but perhaps the middle of the emergency department isn't exactly the right place. So, how about tomorrow night?' he suggested.

'T...tomorrow night?'

'Saturday night. There's a movie showing at the town hall. Haven't you seen the flyers up for it?'

'Uh...yes. Yes.' She eased back, surprised at her reluctance to let go of his fingers. She crossed her arms over her chest but rested one hand over her heart, as though trying to protect it from getting hurt. 'It's an outdoor cinema and everyone sits on rugs and eats food. Yes. I've seen the flyers.' As she spoke she was trying hard to keep her mind off the fact that he was still so incredibly close.

'Let's go together.'

'I'm...I'm on call.' Being alone with Oscar, planning to talk about the sensations he evoked within her... Could she do that? Feelings were to be kept personal, not telling anyone how you really felt because the public façade was more important to maintain for the sake of the family. That was what had been drummed into her by her father and nannies and her brother and everyone else in the social circle she'd been raised in. But she wasn't in those circles any more. She was on the other side of the world and perhaps it was time for her to make new rules for herself.

'I know, but the majority of the district is going to be at this event so if there's going to be any medical emergencies, chances are they'll happen there so we'll be in the right place at the right time.'

'So you want to go to this event together?'

'Yes. And I mean "together", as in a date.'

'A date?' Even the words caused her heart to race. Daisy pursed her lips in an effort to control the riotous sensations of unbelievable dread and excited anticipation that flooded her. 'Oscar! We've spent the past week trying to ignore this chemistry which seems to exist between us and now you want to embrace it?'

'Ignoring it clearly hasn't worked that well for either of us. Don't you think it's worth trying to sort things out? To talk about the "what if"s'?'

Daisy tentatively shook her head. '"What if"s can be dangerous. What if I tell you something that you don't like? How will you treat me after that? What if I confide in you and you let me down and I treat you differently?'

'And what if we figure out what this really is between us and sort it out? If necessary, I'll move out of the residence.'

She frowned at the thought of not seeing him all the time and felt a pang of regret. 'That'll set tongues wagging.'

'So let's discuss it later. Let's sort it out because I've lived in limbo before, Daisy, and I don't much care for it. Talking plainly, figuring things out. That's good.'

'And what if we decide to pursue this…this…'

'Frighteningly natural chemistry which exists between us?'

'Yes. That. What do we do then?'

'We'll figure it out. We're two very intellectual peo-ple, Daisy.' He raised her hand to his lips and brushed a kiss across her knuckles, just as he had every night since Darwin.

'Uh-huh.' She was completely unable to speak.

'And to save us from both tearing each other's clothes off while we discuss such a sensitive topic—'

'Shh.' Even hearing him say those words was starting to cause a warmth to flood throughout her entire body. 'Someone might hear you.'

'Tomorrow night, we'll be able to sit near the back of the crowd, out of the way, and pretend to enjoy the movie while we sort this attraction out.'

She stared at his lips for a long moment before slowly shaking her head in bemusement. 'You've got it all sorted out, eh?'

'Absolutely, mate.' He winked at her and she momen-tarily found it difficult to remember to breathe. Why did he have such a devastating effect on her equilibrium?

Daisy closed her eyes and forced herself to breathe deeply because when he looked at her like that, as though he wanted nothing more than to forget all their responsi-bilities and simply spend the rest of the day kissing her, her mind turned to mush.

'OK.' She kept her eyes closed as she spoke. 'Movies. Tomorrow night. We can talk.'

'Good.' When he brushed a light finger across her cheek, her eyelids snapped open and she quickly pushed his hand away.

'Someone might see.' She looked around but the ED was still very bare. 'Things may be relaxed and informal out here in the middle of nowhere but not for me.'

'And it is for that very reason that I bid you farewell.' He stood and affected a mock bow before turning and walking from the ED. Daisy knew she should follow, knew she had a few patients she needed to see in her afternoon pre-operative clinic, but, due to Oscar's flirting, she was now unable to move her legs.

'Darn that man,' she mumbled. Why did he have to be so incredibly wonderful?

Now he wanted to take her on a date? It seemed so odd to be organising a date with him when they lived in the same house. *Our house.* Even remembering him saying those words was enough to cause a fresh bout of tingles to flood throughout her. Why, oh, why couldn't she control her emotions? And what was she supposed to do when he started asking difficult questions?

Agreeing to go on this date meant she'd need to open up to him, especially as she really did want to figure out where this attraction might lead. She hadn't expected any-thing like this to happen when she'd accepted the job but now that it had… She'd lived a lot of her life not know-ing what was going on, not understanding why her par-ents argued or why she was sent out of the room, or off to boarding school or generally overlooked. Was she ready to tell him more? To tell him about her mother's alco-holism? About how, until her mother decided to get per-manent treatment, Daisy's life would never really be her own? Would that make a difference to Oscar? Would he try and sell the story to the papers, just as her last boy-friend, Walter, had?

What if she and Oscar started a relationship only to have it go sour? What would happen then? He'd clearly been burned before so she doubted he'd want to try that again. Was that what he wanted to talk about? Was he only in-terested in a short-term affair with her? Was she capable of giving him that? Would they be able to share the same house? Work alongside each other? Continue to provide expert care to their patients if things went wrong and they ended up disliking each other?

Daisy leaned her head into her hands and whimpered. What had she done? She couldn't go on a date with Oscar! It was ridiculous. Nice things didn't happen to her. Nice things happened to other people and, as such, she knew she had to put a stop to the ridiculousness that there could ever be anything between herself and Oscar other than a professional working relationship.

She'd seen it happen time and time again in the army, when colleagues had started a relationship only to have it fail and yet they'd been in the middle of a jungle, expected to work together. The tensions in the surgery tents had been hopelessly fraught and had made the working environment unbearable for everyone.

No. She couldn't let that happen here. Not when she'd been accepted as part of the community. No. She and Oscar would remain colleagues with a professional friendship. Nothing more.

With that resolved, she breathed in deeply before standing and straightening her shoulders. Now that she had her priorities straight once more, now that she hadn't let him talk her into doing something she wasn't ready for, she could concentrate on her work. Her patients awaited and, with a firmness to her stride, she headed towards the clinic rooms next door, finally feeling more like herself.

Oscar and the unsettling way he had made her feel were now completely behind her. Once and for all.

CHAPTER TEN

THAT EVENING, IN order to avoid being alone with Oscar in the house, Daisy suggested they go to the pub for dinner. She'd also planned to tell him she couldn't go on the date to the movies with him, that she'd had second thoughts, but they'd been interrupted by a bar-room brawl of epic proportions, with Bazza in the centre of it, and the two of them had spent the next three hours in Emergency, treating the foolhardy farmers who had enjoyed one too many 'knock-off' beers.

On Saturday morning, Daisy had headed off early to her clinic, feeling so incredibly self-conscious about the house space she shared with Oscar. It was happening already, the strange awkwardness she knew would come if they acted upon their attraction. Surely when she told him the date was off, he would understand, as the confused tension that already filled the house seemed to be rapidly increasing.

At the end of her clinic, she finished writing up the notes and then returned them to the filing room. Oscar had told her he had plans to computerise the entire practice but sometimes things took a lot longer to deal with out here in the middle of nowhere. The room she was in was floor-to-ceiling shelves with patient files on either side.

When Oscar walked in to return his own case notes, she

felt his presence before she saw him. Breathing in deeply, she turned around to face him.

'All done?' he asked, putting his armful of case notes on the ground.

'Yes. Just have to file this last set of case notes and I'm done for the day.'

'All ready for our date this evening?' He was edging closer, his gaze dipping to look at her lips before returning to meet her eyes.

'About that—' she began but then realised how he was looking at her. 'Why are you looking at me like that?' she asked, trying not to look back at him, trying instead to concentrate on putting the last set of notes into place, but she was having difficulty due to the trembling that seemed to have flooded through her body at his nearness.

'Let me help you with that.' He put his hand over hers and together they slipped the file into place. The instant he touched her, she gasped and looked up at him. She licked her lips, unable to stop herself, and she was delighted when he didn't let go of her hand but instead drew her closer. 'I have been completely aware of you all day long, from the moment you woke up this morning until right now.'

As he spoke he slid his arms around her waist. 'You're driving me crazy.'

'I know,' she whispered, her heart hammering wildly against her ribs. He shifted in the small area so that he was standing as close to her as possible and, because of the confined space, Daisy slid her hands up to rest on his chest, not sure whether she should push him away or pull him closer.

'You smell so good. Your perfume drives me wild.'

'Mmm-hmm,' she responded, her senses working on overdrive as she breathed in his own glorious scent. 'Likewise.'

'My perfume…' he started bringing his head closer to hers, his words barely above a whisper '…drives you wild?'

'Mmm-hmm,' she repeated, licking her lips again.

'I want to kiss you, Daisy. Really kiss you as I've been longing to do ever since last week when we were in Darwin.'

Even just hearing the words from him was enough to cause a thousand tingles to flood throughout her body, making her tremble with excited anticipation.

'I know we're going to talk tonight, that we're going to figure things out—' He bent his head and brushed a kiss to her cheek. 'But if it turns out we decide just to be friends—'

He slowly shifted around to the other side, his breath mingling with hers as his lips passed hers. He didn't kiss her though; instead, he brushed a kiss to her other cheek and it was all Daisy could do not to sag completely into his arms, her body filled with a want and need that only he could satisfy.

'I don't want to miss this…opportunity.'

No sooner had he said the last word than he gave them both what they so desperately wanted and pressed his lips to hers. Daisy gasped at the contact and then instantly slid her hands further up his chest to wrap them around his neck. Oscar was kissing her. It was what she'd been wanting all morning long, to have him really kiss her, not just the light, teasing tastes they'd shared in Darwin.

His mouth was on hers with a gentleness that only caused more tingles and heightened her awareness of him. She opened her mouth when he nibbled at her lower lip, matching his urgency, needing him to know she wanted this as much as he did.

There were all sorts of logical thoughts springing to her mind, such as what did this kiss mean? What would happen when it was over? What did Oscar want from her? Daisy closed her eyes tighter and pushed those thoughts away. Just because she'd been raised to always consider the logical consequences of her actions, didn't mean she had to follow that rule now.

The way Oscar was making her feel as he deepened the kiss, as he drew her closer to him, as he seemed to ignite every nerve ending in her body, was something she'd never felt before. Good heavens! If she'd known that kissing him was going to be like this then she would have done it that first morning after she'd woken up with thoughts of him in her head.

Now, it was as though being close to him was a drug and one she'd become addicted to in next to no time. Her heart was pounding against her chest with such force that she was positive he could hear it. Her breathing had increased and she knew that if she didn't ease back from the glorious sensations he was creating with his lips pressed so perfectly to her own, she would probably suffocate. At the moment, she couldn't think of a more delicious way to go!

Oscar moved back a bit and looked deeply into her eyes before tucking a stray wisp of hair behind her ear, his fingers both soothing and caressing her skin, causing a fresh round of tingles to spread throughout her. 'What is it?' he asked, looking at her with curiosity.

'Pardon?'

'You're frowning, Daisy.' He brushed his fingers across her forehead, smoothing out the lines, delighted he was allowed to touch her in such a familiar way. His mind and body were still reeling from that kiss. The woman before him was so amazing, so incredible. She came across as all pompous and hoity-toity but in reality she was as vulnerable as the next person.

'I am?' She instantly smiled up at him and he couldn't

resist brushing his lips across hers, deepening the kiss for another moment before actually putting her from him and taking a few steps backwards, almost tripping over the files he'd left on the floor.

'It might be better if I stand over here.'

A cautious look immediately came into her eyes. 'Why? Have I done something wrong?'

'What? No. No.' He shook his head instantly. 'I want nothing more than to hold you close, to kiss you again and again, but if I do I'm not sure I'd be able to stop my urges.'

'You have urges?'

Her words were clipped, her vowels perfectly rounded and where a few weeks ago he would have thought she was making fun of him or simply being thick, he now recognised that small twinkle in her eyes, caught that minute twitch of her lips as the corners curved upwards. She was teasing him and flirting with him and he liked it—a lot. He grinned at her and raised an eyebrow.

'Where you're concerned? Absolutely.' He crossed his arms over his chest as she slowly closed the distance between them. 'Playing with fire, Dr Daisy?'

'I like a bit of danger in my life. It allows me to feel truly alive with every fibre of my being.'

'So now you're saying I'm dangerous?' His words were spoken softly as she now stood toe to toe with him. She was wearing flat shoes today so he was slightly taller than her but in many respects they were still almost eye to eye. He clenched his jaw as her sweet floral scent wound itself around him.

'How is it possible that you can smell as fresh as a daisy all the time?' His gaze dipped to her lips and he swallowed, wanting so badly to pull her back into his arms and kiss her with such abandon that the only conclusion would be to sweep her off her feet and carry her back to their place where they could be truly alone.

But Daisy wasn't 'some woman'. No. Daisy was special. He wanted nothing more than to be with her, to get to know her better, to build a relationship with her, but what would happen when her contract was up? Six months. She'd come here for six months and while there was the possibility she could renew her contract, would she? If things went wrong between them—

Fear suddenly gripped his heart. He'd been down this road before. It was the whole reason why they were supposed to be discussing things tonight, but he hadn't been able to stop himself from pressing his lips to hers, from seeing whether this attraction between them really was as incredible as he thought it might be. It was...*more* so than he could ever have imagined.

'Are we taking it in turns to frown? Because you seem incredibly lost in thought,' she said quietly as she reached out and touched her fingers gently to his forehead, reciprocating his earlier action.

Oscar uncrossed his arms and took her hands in his, mainly to stop her from touching him, because that one simple caress was enough to start unravelling the tight control on his emotions he was trying to maintain.

'I like what's happening between us, Daisy.'

Her smile was instant—and delightful. 'So do I.' She shrugged one shoulder. 'I was going to tell you I couldn't go to the movies with you tonight, that deciding to spend more time together—in a personal sense—was probably a bad move and one we might end up regretting.'

He chuckled. 'I think we're both over-thinkers.'

Daisy relaxed at this, seeing that he, too, had his concerns. 'Oh, good.'

Oscar chuckled again and shook his head before leaning

forward to press his lips to hers, unable to resist kissing her after she'd sounded so formal, pompous and nervous all at the same time. When she started to deepen the kiss, he put his hands onto her shoulders and eased her back. 'I really should put my files away and then go help out in the ED.'

'Yes. Yes.' She cleared her throat. 'I really should go and start house calls.'

'And I should really tell everyone what I just saw!'

Oscar and Daisy instantly turned towards the doorway where Tori stood, gaping at them with a goofy grin on her face. 'How long has this been going on?' She waggled her finger at the two of them as she walked towards her desk.

'About ten minutes,' Oscar said as they both came out of the file room. He placed a protective arm around Daisy's shoulders, pleased when she didn't shrug him away or deny what was happening between them.

'Well...I think it's been building up for quite a few weeks,' Daisy added, smiling at him. That one look gave Oscar courage. She was invested in...whatever this was that existed between them.

'Do you think you might be able to keep it on the down-low, at least until after the movie tonight?' he asked Tori.

'Are you kidding me?' Tori spread her arms wide. 'The whole district has just been waiting for the two of you to realise how perfect you are for each other. In fact, Erica's been running a betting pool on it.'

'Huh.' Oscar thought for a moment. 'Are you in the betting pool?'

Tori's eyes widened as the reality of the situation dawned on her. 'Ooh. I could make a lot of money here. Who else knows about the two of you?'

Oscar shook his head and slipped his arm off Daisy's shoulders, taking her hand in his. 'Come on, Daisy. We'll do house calls together and leave crazy Tori to take care of the ED by herself.'

'It's quiet anyway,' Tori called after them as they left the clinic, heading out to walk in the sunshine. It was then that Daisy started to feel an enormous weight lift from her shoulders. She couldn't remember the last time she'd done something just for herself.

The fact that they did the house calls together certainly raised a few more eyebrows and really set the tongues to wagging. Daisy was certain that by that night's movie session the entire community would have settled their bets.

'We are most definitely the talk of the town,' Oscar said to her as they headed home to shower and change for the evening's festivities. 'I wouldn't be surprised if they all cheer and clap when we arrive together, hand in hand.' He took her hand in his and gave it a little squeeze.

Daisy smiled at him, caught up in the brightness of his eyes. She wasn't sure if she would ever get tired of gazing into them. Oscar really was such a handsome man and one who seemed to understand her completely. It seemed odd that they'd only known each other for such a short time and yet it seemed as though she'd been waiting for him her whole life. He'd gently but firmly smashed down the walls she'd erected over the years to protect herself and now he looked at her as though she were the most beautiful, wonderful and incredible woman in the world. How could any woman not be affected by that?

She started to laugh, unable to stop the giggles.

'What?'

'It's nothing.'

'You're just laughing for no reason now?'

Daisy couldn't help it. Her smile increased and she giggled again. 'It's just that…well…I'm happy.'

His smile was wide and bright and he leaned forward

to kiss her. 'I'm sure you deserve to be.' He opened the door to their residence. 'After you, Lady Daisy.' He affected a small bow.

Annoyance hard and fast burned through her, destroying her happiness as though someone had smashed a glass window with a hammer. 'Please don't call me that.' Even she heard the haughtiness of her tone and when Oscar gave her a puzzled smile, she shook her head. 'Sorry. I didn't mean to sound so snappy.'

'It's OK.' As they headed into the cool of the house Oscar sensed it wasn't the right time to press her for answers. Oscar was taken with her, even though he'd done his best to fight it. He knew he needed to ease the tension he could see in her shoulders and he quickly started talking about the food everyone would bring to tonight's barbecue.

'We're bringing a salad,' he said. 'So chop-chop, Dr Daisy. Literally,' he said, handing her a bunch of carrots. Slowly, as they worked side by side, the tension in her shoulders began to ease and the smile began to reach her eyes once more.

Oscar continued to chat, to tell her about the delicious goodies other people in the town would bring.

'Glenys is making her famous all natural ice-blocks. My favourite is peach and blueberry.'

'Ice-blocks?'

Oscar nodded. 'Of course. Being from England, you wouldn't often eat ice-blocks, now, would you?'

'Hey!' She scolded. 'It gets hot over there. Not as hot as here, but it still gets hot enough that we eat iced lollies.'

'Well, you'll love these. Glenys purées fruit, mixes it together and then freezes it in her moulds so you have the perfect ice-block on a stick with no added nasties. It's like perfect sunshine in an ice-block. You love strawberries, right?'

'How do you know that?'

'Uh…because I've seen you eat them and you seem to savour them in the same way that my sister used to eat chocolate.'

'Oh.' She'd had no idea he'd been observing her. She couldn't blame him though, as she'd been observing him as well. She knew he didn't like mushrooms but was more than happy to cook them for her in the morning when he made breakfast. She knew he drank his coffee black with two sugars and she knew he had a marvellous baritone voice because he often sang in the shower.

They talked a bit more about the fruit ice-blocks Glenys made and the home-made lamingtons Erica would be bringing and by the time they were changed and ready to walk down to the town hall, Daisy's stomach was already grumbling.

True to Oscar's description, there were tables laden with food, the ceiling fans and air conditioner in the hall working overtime as they all joined together, laughing and eating and having a brilliant time.

Naturally, Daisy and Oscar were subjected to a lot of knowing looks and smiles and pats on the back and handshakes regarding the change in their relationship from colleagues to…more than colleagues.

Even Daisy wasn't one hundred per cent sure what was going on between them. They'd kissed. They'd held hands. They didn't seem in any hurry to be separated from each other and she liked that he appeared to enjoy being around her all the time. However, deep down inside, she knew it would come to an end. Things always did for her. Nothing ever worked out the way she envisioned it and the fact that they were living in the same house, working at the same hospital and now attending functions together meant that, sooner rather than later, she half expected Oscar to get sick of her company.

'Ready to come and sit outside and watch the movie?' Oscar asked her after the sun had gone down. Police officer Henry and a gaggle of others had set up a large screen behind the town hall in order to screen the movie. The flies had all disappeared and the mosquitoes seemed to be giving them the night off, even though several people, including Daisy, sprayed themselves with repellent.

'Well, I do declare,' Oscar stated as he came to sit beside her on the rug he'd spread for them. 'You are becoming quite the local, Dr Daisy.' They were sitting near the back of the gathered group, some people sitting on beanbags and others having carried sofas and rocking chairs down to the hall from their own houses. Daisy was pleased with the community feel, delighted at the acceptance she felt and thrilled that Oscar thought she was turning into a local.

'You're all set. Got your repellent on. Using your event programme as a makeshift fan to cool yourself down and relaxing back on a rug finishing off an ice-block.'

'This was my third,' she said softly, whispering her words near his ear. 'You were right. They're delicious.'

Her face was tilted towards him, her lips slightly parted, as though begging him to kiss her. He didn't disappoint and captured her mouth with his. 'Mmm... Strawberry and apple,' he remarked after tasting her cool lips. 'My favourite.'

'I thought you liked peach and blueberry.'

'I wasn't talking about the ice-block,' he murmured and captured her lips once more in another kiss, this one slow and teasing and igniting the need deep inside Daisy she was finding difficult to ignore. He then shifted closer to her and was delighted when she leaned her head on his shoulder as they watched the movie with the rest of the town.

After the first hour, Daisy eased back, lying propped up on one arm. She'd seen this movie several times before and loved the storyline of how the main protagonists had to work together to solve the mystery...falling in love as the story progressed.

'If only life were that simple,' she whispered, and as he heard the pain in her words his protective instinct began to flare. Who had hurt his Daisy? And would she ever trust him enough to tell him about it?

CHAPTER ELEVEN

'WHAT DID YOU think of the movie?' Tori asked. 'I know most people have seen it as it's a classic but there's just something about sitting out here together as a community and watching it as one big happy family,' she continued, not giving Daisy a chance to answer.

'Oh, I doubt she and Oscar were watching much of the movie,' Glenys remarked as she walked past. 'Too busy canoodling, from what I could see.' She laughed as she carried her picnic rug and chairs to her car.

'Don't mind Glenys,' Tori said as Oscar finished folding up their own picnic rug. 'The gossip is always rampant when something new and exciting happens in town.'

'Was Scotty here tonight?' Oscar asked but Tori shook her head.

'He's still in Darwin with Gracie and her parents, helping out. He calls me regularly with updates.' The nurse seemed very pleased that she and Scotty were back on speaking terms.

'That's right. I thought he was coming back in time for the movie night.'

'No. Gracie's doing well, as you both know, but her parents still rely on Scotty to help them out.'

'Of course. Anyway,' Oscar stated, slipping his hand into Daisy's, 'time to get some sleep, I think. Who knows what sort of emergency we'll encounter next?' It was just after midnight as they headed back to the doctors' residence and Daisy was having a hard time controlling her yawns. 'Do you realise, my delicious Daisy...' she chuckled at his name for her '...that when you're tired and sleepy you're even more irresistible?'

'I am?'

'Yes. I remember that very first night you arrived. I watched over you as you slept, making sure your temperature didn't spike.'

'You did?'

'Of course I did. I couldn't have my new doctor checking out before she'd really checked in.' He pulled her into his arms and looked into her eyes. 'I love that you're almost the same height as me. I love the way you throw yourself into whatever situation you face, family, war zones or outback problems. You just...confront whatever is in your own way and I admire that quality in you.'

'Admire it, please, but don't love me, Oscar.' She closed her eyes and rested her forehead against his. 'Don't love me,' she whispered.

Initially, he'd only used the word as a throwaway line, in a non-serious context, but seeing her reaction caused him to question further. 'Why not? You'd be so easy to love.' And he meant it, he realised. The knowledge should have scared him but, instead, he felt a peace settle over him that holding Daisy close to his heart was the right thing to do.

'I wouldn't be easy to love because my life is not a normal one,' she stated, pain in her tone, but she was more than happy for him to capture her mouth with his, more than happy to lose herself to the sensations he could evoke within her. She tried so hard to kiss him back the same way, to let him know that he made her happy, that she thoroughly enjoyed being with him but...love? How could she possibly know what love was when she wasn't sure she'd ever received it from anyone else?

'What's love got to do with it?' her father had ranted when she'd begged him to help her mother, the woman he was supposed to cherish and care about.

'You don't love Mother?' she'd questioned.

'I'm exceedingly fond of her, Daisy, but love is for people with no real power. We have position, integrity and breeding to uphold. Your mother's antics are disgraceful and, as such, she should deal with them and not drag me down to her level. She can host my parties, but apart from that she can keep out of my way until she can get herself under control. She's so weak.' He'd said the last three words with such distaste and at that moment, Daisy had hated her father. He had no compassion, no understanding. All he cared about was how the situation looked to the outside world. It was why he'd been more than happy for her to study medicine because bragging to his friends that his daughter was a qualified doctor had been impressive.

'Love only brings pain,' her mother had said when Daisy had once more tried to get her into a rehabilitation facility. Cecilia had already been to one in Spain and for almost a year it had worked. She'd been strong and kept off the alcohol, but when she'd discovered Daisy's father was having an affair with the woman who had purported to be Cecilia's best friend she'd returned to the bottle.

Love only brings pain. The words kept repeating over and over in Daisy's head. Her parents were living proof that the statement was true.

If she dared to allow herself to love Oscar, to really love Oscar, would it bring her pain? Every time she'd tried to love the people in her life, her parents, her brother, her friends…it had indeed brought her nothing but pain. So she'd held herself aloof, wanting to concentrate on her work, on using the skills she'd gained in order to help others. That had certainly brought a sense of satisfaction but here with Oscar, here in his arms, in their lounge room, she wasn't sure she could take those final steps towards supposed happiness.

She broke free, her breathing ragged as she looked into his eyes. 'Oscar, where is this going?'

'Well…' He raised his eyebrows suggestively. 'Your room's probably cleaner than mine.'

'No, not that. Of course I realise that on an attraction level, on a sensual level, we are indeed compatible, but what's next? We sleep together? What then? We work closely together. The health and well-being of this town rests on our shoulders. We were scheduled to have this discussion this evening and yet all we've done is ignore the conversation we really should have been having.'

'Daisy.' He kissed her forehead, then led her over to the lounge, which contained the two wing-back chairs. They sat down together, Oscar holding both of her hands in his. He paused for a moment, then spoke clearly but quietly. 'I've been hurt twice before, my heart ripped up into little pieces, and I swore to myself it would never happen again.'

'And yet tonight you mentioned love,' she felt compelled to point out.

'I know. It stunned me as much as it stunned you but, at the end of the day, the heart wants what it wants even if logically the decision isn't a sound one.'

'You'd risk getting hurt for a third time?'

'If it meant I had memories with you?' He thought about it for a moment then nodded. 'I think I would.'

'But…there's still so much about me you don't know, so much that I haven't told you.'

'I know enough.'

'Really? You'd still feel the same way about me if I told you that my family is very wealthy?'

'Are they?'

'Yes.'

'Good for them.'

Daisy let go of his hands and took a few steps away from him. 'Oscar, my father is an earl. He's Lord Forsythe-York. My mother is Lady Forsythe-York.'

'Titled, eh?'

She spread her arms wide at his blasé attitude. 'How can you not care about this?'

'Because it doesn't change the person *you* are right now, the woman standing in front of me, the woman who paid for Mrs Piper's surgery.'

'You know about that?'

'Timothy told me when we were in Darwin. All it did was make me admire you more.'

'So it wouldn't bother you that my official title is Lady Daisy Philomena Sarah Forsythe-York?'

'Ah.' It was as though a light bulb clicked on over his head. '*That's* why you didn't like it when I called you Lady Daisy. Fair enough, too.' He grinned at her. 'Pretty name. So you really are a lady?'

'I am.'

'And you have certain societal responsibilities that your family expect you to uphold?'

'I do.'

'And yet you've stood your ground and demanded that you go to medical school. You worked overseas, you joined the army and went to war! Daisy, you're amazing and brilliant and brave and so many other things that this news doesn't change my opinion of you at all.'

Daisy threw her arms up in the air. 'Why are you being so accepting and complacent about this?'

'I'm not being complacent, Daisy, I assure you. The last time we had a big turnout to a movie night like that was about three weeks before Lucinda passed away. Tonight brought back many memories of her telling me to find myself again, to not let myself be squashed by my mistakes of the past, to enjoy the life I had. "Life is for living, little brother—so live it…for yourself and for me." That's what she said and tonight I remembered that. Tonight, I experienced what those words meant. Sitting there with you, watching the movie with the town, I don't know…I felt—' He shrugged one shoulder. 'I felt happy.'

'And you haven't felt that way in a long time?'

He nodded. 'See? We're not so different, Daisy.'

'Yes, we are! How can I make you understand the very real differences between us?'

'You like strawberries. I hate mushrooms. Yes, we're different, but that's also what makes us unique. However, when we are together, when I hold you in my arms…' He stood and started walking slowly towards her. She stood her ground, wanting him to be near to her but also wanting to find a way to get it through his thick head that they came from completely different backgrounds.

'Oscar.' She put up one hand to stop him advancing but all he did was take it in his and kiss it. 'Your parents passed away when you were young. You were raised by your sister. You've had pain and loss all throughout your life.'

'I know this.'

'If you insist on becoming involved with me, then you'll continue to have pain and loss.'

'I disagree,' he murmured, cupping her face and lowering his head to capture her lips. He was rewarded with a sigh and her arms entwining around his neck. How could she say this was wrong? How could she say that what existed between them was only going to bring pain and loss?

'Something that feels this right,' he whispered against her mouth, 'couldn't possibly be that wrong.'

'Shut up and kiss me,' she demanded and he grinned before complying with her wishes. It was only the ringing of her cell phone that stopped them. At this hour of the night, it was imperative they answer all calls.

'Emergency?' She extracted herself from his embrace and walked to the table beside the wing-back chair where she'd left her phone.

'You get the phone. I'll get the emergency bag.' He spun on his heel and headed towards the kitchen. He heard her answer the call, 'Dr Daisy speaking,' and couldn't help but smile that she was now calling herself that. She was becoming more of an honorary Aussie every day. Not that he wanted her to lose her haughty Britishness, as he loved that part of her.

Loved. There was that word again. Until tonight, he hadn't allowed himself to think of her in such a way, but since they'd given in to the need to touch and caress and kiss, he hadn't been able to stop the word from springing to mind...or his lips.

'Don't love me,' she'd said, and yet she'd still to give him a decent reason as to why not.

Oscar grabbed the emergency bag then went back into the lounge room to find out what the situation was. What he found was Daisy sitting in the chair, her face almost deathly pale, just hanging up the phone.

'Daisy?' He received no reply from her. 'Daisy?' His senses heightened to full alert. 'Daisy, what's wrong? What is it?' He knelt down in front of her and stared into her face.

Slowly she looked at him but her eyes were glassy, not seeing him at all. 'It's my mother. She's in a coma.'

CHAPTER TWELVE

'WHAT?' OSCAR STARED at her, then gathered her close, or at least he tried to. This time when she put up her hand, she kept it up, using her strength to push him away.

'Don't hug me.'

'What?' he said again. 'Why not? I'm here for you. I'll do whatever you need.'

'I need you not to hug me.' Her words were clipped, her expression was controlled and, although she still had very little colour in her face, her eyes were huge and expressive. It showed her concern, her worries, her fears. 'If you hug me,' she continued a moment later, 'I'll crumble and right now I don't need to crumble, I need to be one hundred per cent in control of my faculties.'

'All right.' He held up his hands but still stayed kneeling in front of her. 'No hugging. What can I do to help you?' For a while he thought she wasn't going to answer him, her eyes still staring unseeingly past him, her mind clearly working fast. Her mask, the one he'd seen her wear that very first day she'd arrived here in Meeraji Lake, came back into place. She had herself under control. If that was what she needed in order to function, then so be it.

'A cup of tea, please.'

'As you wish,' he stated and immediately stood and headed into the kitchen. While the kettle boiled, he could hear her on the phone and realised she was making a few calls of her own. When he returned with her cup of tea, she was just dialling a new number.

'Thank you,' she remarked and eased back in the chair, pulling her feet beneath her, protecting herself and at the same time shutting him out. He remembered when she'd first arrived and how she hadn't wanted to accept anyone's help, how she'd wanted to get better all on her own. That woman, the one who had survived terrible situations in the heart of a war-torn country, came to the fore. Still, he wasn't just going to walk away and leave her alone. Whether she liked it or not, he was going to stand by her.

'John,' she said a moment later into the phone. 'I wanted you to give me an update.' Her beautiful eyes swam with tears as she listened to her brother. 'John! Mother is in hospital. I've just received a call from her physician to tell me she's in a coma. How can you not know this?' A pause. 'I don't care if you're in Scotland. I'm on the other side of the world and it will take you far less time to get to her than me.'

As Oscar listened unashamedly to her side of the conversation, equally astonished at her brother's lack of concern, he started to realise what she'd been trying to tell him earlier, about how her family was very different from his.

'Get on a plane. Drive in your car. I don't care. Just get to the hospital.' Another pause. 'I'm presuming Father knows as he's the one who's no doubt caused all this with his constant berating and emotional bullying of her.' Daisy gritted her teeth. 'No, I'm not going to call him and, yes, you *do* have to go.' She closed her eyes. 'Because she's your mother, John. Think of how it will look if the papers get a hold of this story. You'll be the doting son. The one at her bedside. Helping her through this situation.'

Her family were newsworthy? He guessed an earl's wife

being admitted to hospital in a coma might very well be newsworthy. Apparently Daisy's latest attempt to shift her brother into gear had worked because she sighed and opened her eyes. 'Thank you, John. I've booked a flight but I still won't be there for another two days—at the earliest.'

'You've already booked your flight?' Oscar asked after she'd hung up.

'Of course.' Daisy stood and headed to her bedroom, where she got out her suitcase and put it on the bed.

'Do you need to pack right now?' he asked.

'Yes. I've called Henry and he's organising for the emergency chopper to fly me to Darwin. I'm booked on the mid-morning flight to Heathrow airport.'

'Then I'm going with you.'

She stopped and stared at him as though he'd grown an extra head. 'You're going to come to England with me?' Her tone was laced with sarcasm and he so desperately wanted to tell her that that was exactly what he was going to do; however, both of them knew that was impossible.

'I can go with you to Darwin. I can check on Gracie while I'm there.'

'Oscar, I don't think that's wise.'

'I don't care what you think,' he stated and pulled his own phone from his pocket and called Tori to let her know that he and Daisy would be leaving to go to Darwin so she was first point of call for any emergencies.

'There.' He shoved his phone back into his pocket. 'All organised. I'm just as stubborn as you, remember?'

Daisy's answer was to grit her teeth and toss more of her clothes into her suitcase. For a woman who was usually meticulous, she didn't seem to care all that much about the contents of her suitcase. 'How will you get back from Darwin?' she asked. 'I've told Henry I'll pay the cost of the chopper taking me to Darwin. Are you going to pay for your own ride home?'

'I can hitch a ride with the RFDS, as you well know,' he stated. 'I'm not backing down, Daisy. You need to go and see your mother. I understand that but your attitude of trying to shut me out, of making it seem as though this situation has nothing to do with me—'

'It doesn't have anything to do with you,' she interrupted, raising her tone. 'This is *my* family. *My* life.'

'I thought things had changed between us. I thought we'd moved past this professional acquaintance, past being just friends.' He opened his arms wide, almost wanting her to see that this was him, stripped raw, willing to throw himself at her feet. 'Daisy. You know how I feel about you. Let me help.'

'There's nothing you can do.' She enunciated every word meticulously and he dropped his arms back to his sides. 'Excuse me.' She sidestepped him and removed the clothes from her closet.

'OK. If that's the way you want to play it, I'll help you pack. Let me get your toiletries for you.'

Daisy glanced at him, clearly wondering if he was now trying to get rid of her, but thankfully she could see his genuineness and started to soften a little towards him. For one split second, Oscar thought he might have reached her, might have broken through that tough diplomatic exterior she was wont to wear, but as fleetingly as it came, it disappeared.

'Thank you.' She continued to pack and Oscar knew his only course of action was to stand his ground, to not let her quash his efforts to become a part of her life. He wasn't even sure when he'd realised he *needed* to be a part of her life—no matter what. He would even leave Meeraji Lake and move to England if it meant he could be with her and he most certainly hadn't felt that way with either of his previous relationships. All he knew right now was that he needed to support her and if she couldn't tell him what she needed from him, then he would do his best and muddle through.

He returned with her things and handed them to her. 'Thank you,' she replied again, ever polite, and as he watched her move about the room in a stiff and controlled manner he realised, for the first time, that he was actually looking at Lady Daisy Philomena Sarah Forsythe-York. Here she was. The groomed aristocrat…and he still loved her. It didn't matter whether she was Dr Daisy, Major Daisy or Lady Daisy, at the end of the day, she was *his* Daisy.

'What wrenches my heart,' he murmured as she zipped the suitcase closed, 'is that you think you need to go through all of this alone. You don't, Daisy.'

'I do.'

'No.' He caressed her cheek, pushing her hair behind her ear. 'You don't. I'm here. I'm here for you. In whatever capacity you require.' He cupped her cheek, wanting to exude as much love and support as he could. When she didn't immediately pull away from his touch, he leaned forward and kissed her, wanting to let her *feel* just how much he cared for her.

'Oscar.' His name was a whisper of pain, then she eased away from him and shook her head. 'Don't come to Darwin with me.'

'Daisy, I—'

She held up her hand. Didn't he understand how difficult this was for her? Couldn't he see the extra pain he was causing her?

'Can you at least tell me why? Why don't you want me to come with you?'

'Because saying goodbye to you here is hard enough.'

It was then that her voice broke and tears filled her eyes. 'I've been so happy. I want to keep those memories. Please? Please, Oscar?' she pleaded and he knew he'd give in, knew he'd give her whatever she wanted even if it almost killed him to do so. 'I want these last memories to be happy ones, not ones of us arguing.'

He frowned for a moment. 'Daisy, this isn't goodbye.'

'Oscar, my mother is in a coma. Her physician couldn't tell me much over the phone in case his phone is tapped.'

'Tapped? What sort of world do you live in?'

'One very different from here.' Her words were sad and she hefted her suitcase from the bed and started wheeling it towards the front door.

'Can I at least drive you to the helicopter?' he asked as he took the suitcase from her, which, thankfully, she allowed him to do. Again, she shook her head.

'Henry's giving me a lift.'

Oscar couldn't believe his life had gone from happiness to misery in such a short space of time. 'Will you at least call me? Let me know you arrived safely?'

She nodded. 'Kiss me, Oscar. Kiss me goodbye.' She wrapped her arms around his neck, pain filling her eyes. 'Make it memorable.'

'I'll make it memorable, all right, but this isn't goodbye, Daisy.' He gathered her close, knowing she was concerned for her mother, knowing she was going to have a hectic few days of travel ahead of her, knowing she was going to be standing alone, fighting the battles yet to come by herself. He wanted to pour the love, a love that seemed to be increasing with every passing second, into her, wanted to shower it over it, to protect her, to let her know that he was always with her, loving her.

He kissed her with purpose, with reason, with promise until a car horn beeped from outside and Daisy pulled away, slightly breathless. 'I love you, Daisy.'

She shook her head slowly as though she didn't really believe him. 'I'll call you when I'm safely in England.'

'Thank you.' She was so polite, almost impersonal, and he wouldn't have believed it if it hadn't been for her slightly swollen lips, which let him know that she'd enjoyed those kisses as much as him. 'I'd better go. I don't want to keep Henry waiting. Stay inside. Please.'

He pursed his lips for a moment before nodding and forcing a little smile. 'OK, but only because you asked so nicely.' With that, he winked at her and she forced a smile of her own in return.

'Goodbye, Oscar.'

'See you later,' he responded in the typical Australian farewell. Within another moment, she'd walked out of the door and closed it behind her. Another moment later, he heard Henry's police car pull away and drive off into the distance.

How long he stood there, he had no clue. All he knew was that the house smelled like Daisy, like the woman he loved, and although she'd thought she was saying goodbye to him, she had another think coming.

CHAPTER THIRTEEN

'Have you heard from Daisy?' Tori asked him two days later as they dealt with a busier than usual emergency department.

'She called to say she's arrived.'

'Any news on her mother?'

'She didn't give me any details.'

'Have you tried calling her?'

'Yes, Tori, I have,' he snapped. 'She probably hasn't been able to get back to me because she's at the hospital looking after her mother.'

'Do you know what happened to put her mother into the coma?'

'Just stop with the all the questions and go and see the patient in room two.' He picked up a set of case notes. 'I'll be in room one.' He stalked off to deal with his patient, wishing everyone would stop asking him about Daisy.

It would be fine if the woman would answer his calls, and if she didn't have the time to do that she could at least send him a text message, or email him but Daisy seemed intent on maintaining her radio silence, as it were.

A week later, there was still no news, not from Daisy. Scotty had returned from Darwin, giving them a firsthand account of Gracie's progress and even showing Oscar photographs he'd taken with his cell phone of the wound site.

'That is a great improvement,' he said, handing Scotty's phone back to him.

'Timothy, her doctor, said she's going to make a full recovery although there may be a slight restriction in the movement of her little and ring fingers.'

'Fantastic news. And her parents? Are they home yet?'

'They're going to stay in Darwin until Gracie can be transferred here to Meeraji Lake. It'll make it easier on them.' Scotty continued to talk about his experiences in Darwin but Oscar wasn't listening. Whenever he wasn't with a patient, a part of his thoughts was on Daisy, wondering why she hadn't called him, wondering how her mother was progressing, trying to figure out what her father could possibly have done to send her mother into a coma. Whatever it was, had they managed to keep it out of the papers?

Another week later, he still had no answers and was even more worried than before. He'd been determined that when she'd left, it hadn't been forever, that it wasn't a real 'goodbye', but with the way she seemed to be refusing to return his calls, was ignoring his emails and generally snubbing him, he was starting to wonder whether she hadn't been right.

Was this the end of his relationship with Daisy? Was he willing to let this one go?

'No!' He paced around his house, the house that seemed to be far too empty. Now, when he dreamed about having a wife and children, filling this house with laughter, his wife's face was clear and distinct because it belonged to Daisy.

Whatever he'd felt for Magda or Deidre was nothing compared to how Daisy made him feel. She was his other half, his soulmate. So why was she insistent on causing both of them so much pain?

Another two weeks later, with absolutely no contact,

and he was finally starting to believe that last kiss had really been their goodbye kiss. The only correspondence he'd received from Daisy was her letter of resignation. It stated that due to a family emergency she would be unable to fulfil the full terms of her contract, that she was willing to pay any damages and that he should get in contact with her attorney to settle the details.

Didn't she realise, it wasn't about the money? Did she think that she could just buy him off? What sort of person kissed him the way she had and then left without a word? She thought she had to go through this crisis alone and even though he'd tried to reassure her, to let her know that he was here for her, she'd still rejected him.

It was that that hurt the most, the lack of trust, the disbelief that he could support her, that he would do anything for her. How could she do this to him? How could she kiss him in such a way that clearly indicated she'd had very strong feelings for him, and then just cut him off without another word?

What added fuel to his already annoyed and burning fire were the whispers that seemed to stop the instant he walked into a room. His friends would smile at him, in that sad, pathetic way they had in the past when Deidre had left.

'Poor Oscar,' he'd heard them whisper. 'That's *three* women who have rejected him now. I can't understand why. He's such a nice, handsome bloke.'

Three women. One had left him because he didn't earn enough money. The other had left him because her career was more important and the last... He shook his head. She'd left him because she was stubborn and that was just plain stupid. Daisy was stupid and he was stupid too because he still loved her, even more than when she'd left.

As he sat in the kitchen, drinking a hot cup of tea even though it was still very warm outside, he allowed the pain from his breaking heart to fill his entire body. When someone knocked at the door, he wasn't sure he had the energy to tell them to go away.

'Hello?' Tori called and a moment later she and Scotty walked in together, followed by Glenys, Erica and Henry. 'Are we disturbing your dinner or aren't you bothering to eat food any more?'

'What do you all want?' He sighed and finished his cup of tea, clattering the cup down onto the saucer.

'This is an intervention,' Scotty said, resting his hand on Oscar's shoulder.

'We care about you too much to see you going through this again,' Glenys remarked.

'So,' Erica said with glee, 'we've bought you a ticket to England.'

'A what?' Oscar looked at them all as though they'd gone stark raving bonkers.

'A plane ticket. For you to go to England.' Tori spoke to him as though he were five years old.

'We all chipped in,' Henry remarked as he handed over the piece of paper that indeed confirmed that Oscar was booked to travel overseas the day after tomorrow.

'It's a nice gesture but I can't go.'

'Why not?' Tori asked.

'Why not?' He stood and spread his arms wide. 'Because unless you can find another doctor hiding somewhere in this building, I can't go. I can't leave Meeraji Lake without a doctor for that length of time and Daisy knows it. She knows I won't come after her and therefore she can maintain her resolve not to speak to me because I can't do anything about it except get frustrated and annoyed and—' He stopped and covered his face with his hands.

'But that's where you're wrong,' Scotty said.

'He's right. I've managed to find a locum for you,' Tori

stated. 'Her name is Harriette and she's arriving tomorrow so you'll have a one-day hand-over before you head off on your overseas adventure to bring our Daisy back home.'

'What?' Oscar dropped his hands from his face and stared at the smiling, nodding faces of his friends.

'It's true,' Erica said.

Glenys clapped her hands with excitement. 'Daisy's going to be so surprised to see you.'

Oscar stared at the travel details as the reality of his situation slowly sank in. He was booked to go overseas. A locum would look after the town. He could go and see Daisy.

The question was, would she want to see him?

The phone from the gatehouse buzzed and Daisy walked across the polished marble floors to answer it. She'd been back in England for four weeks and she couldn't believe how oppressed she felt. Her time in Australia, in Meer-aji Lake, seemed like a mirage, something she could see, could remember, but would never be able to touch again.

Her mother, thank goodness, had woken from the coma the day after Daisy had arrived back in England and was now convalescing at home, under Daisy's watchful eye. Daisy's father was home but keeping his distance from the situation as best he could. Upon arriving home, Daisy had discovered her father had insisted upon installing his mistress permanently at the house, that he expected her mother to be civil to the mistress but keep up appearances that everything was perfect in the Forsythe-York house-hold. It had been the last straw for Cecilia and she'd taken to the bottle as though it were her only hope.

Daisy had thrown herself into doing everything she could for her mother, organising for a private nurse as well as handling the press when she'd needed to, and she'd done it all with the firm intention of not focusing on Oscar. She hadn't allowed herself to think about him and how much she missed him because she knew, if she did, she'd end up in a state almost as bad as her mother's. Oscar Price and the way he'd made her feel were in the past. She'd been used to disappointment her entire life so why should now be any different?

She picked up the phone. 'Yes, Gibson?'

'Sorry to bother you, Lady Daisy, but there's an Australian gentleman here who says he knows you. Says he's a doctor, not a reporter. He's becoming more and more agitated the longer I refuse to let him through. He demanded that I ring up to the main house to speak to you.'

'Give me that phone,' Daisy heard a familiar deep voice say and a moment later he spoke.

'Daisy? Daisy, is that you?'

'Oscar! What are you doing here?'

'Not getting past your bulldog. Let me in.'

The last three words were ground between clenched teeth and she had the sense that if she didn't give Gibson the all clear to let Oscar come up to the main house, Oscar would probably find a way to jump the fence and trip every alarm in the place. Then the police would be called, not to mention Gibson and the rest of his security staff weighing in on the misdemeanour. In other words, a complete nightmare.

'Daisy!'

'All right. All right.' A moment later, Gibson came back on the line and she told him to allow Oscar access. The moment she put the phone down, her entire body began to tingle with confusion, excitement and dread. If Oscar was here, then there would be no way she would be able to protect him, to shield him from the overbearing attitude of her family, to ensure her father didn't spend hours interrogating him. Why had he come? What could he possibly hope to gain from—?

The front doorbell rang and she quickly headed across the entry hall, calling to the butler that it was all right, she'd answer the door.

'What are you doing here?' she demanded as soon as she'd opened the large wooden door and stared at Oscar standing opposite her. She hadn't meant to be so direct, so rude, but he'd caught her completely off guard and...and... how could a man look so amazing, so handsome, so...? Her brain shut down and she could think of nothing else except the way his mouth was enticing her to taste, to...to...

And then, as though unable to restrain himself at all, Oscar stepped forward, dropped his bag and gathered her into his arms, pressing his mouth firmly to hers. Daisy wound her arms around his neck and kissed him back with abandon.

Even though he was groggy from the exceedingly long flight, tired, angry and frustrated, all that disappeared in an instant. Daisy. *His* Daisy. She was all he needed and he could stand here kissing her forever.

'Wait. Stop. No.' Daisy wrenched herself free and took two huge steps back from him. 'What are you doing here?' she asked again. Her breathing was as erratic as his and he stepped closer, needing her.

'I would have thought that was obvious.' When he reached for her again, she held up both her hands and he stopped.

'You can't be here.'

'Well, I am.'

'Oscar!'

'Daisy!'

'Shh.' She looked around them, knowing they were probably being observed, whether by the butler, who reported everything to her father, or one of the maids, who, although having signed non-disclosure agreements, wouldn't be above making money off this story. Closing her eyes for a moment, Daisy reached out and grabbed his hand, dragging him through the high-ceilinged rooms, around a few twists and turns, heading further back into the estate home, which was most definitely a mansion.

'Where are we—?'

'Shh!' She put a finger over her lips for emphasis, then opened a door and dragged him inside. He looked around the room, the walls covered with display cabinets containing pieces of patterned china and other ornaments.

'Whoa.' He quickly looked around the room as she let go of his hand and went to close the door. 'I wouldn't want to be the person responsible for dusting this room.'

'Oscar. You shouldn't have come.'

'Then you should have returned my calls, responded to my emails.'

'I thought it best to make a clean break.'

'You thought wrong.' He stepped forward and kissed her again, loving the way she responded to him, as though the time they'd spent apart had done nothing to decrease the attraction between them, but had intensified it instead. When they broke apart, she shook her head and walked over to sit in the only chair in the entire room.

It was an old fashioned tête-à-tête seat, designed in the eighteen hundreds. He sat on one side and Daisy sat on the other. Their faces were incredibly close and he couldn't help but breathe in her scent.

'How's your mother? Is she out of the coma? Improving?' He hoped all the answers were in the affirmative because if things had gone tragically wrong…

'Yes. She's home now, upstairs in fact and starting to eat.'

'She wasn't eating?'

'Not really.' Daisy looked down at her hands, knowing that now he was here he would find out the truth. Even by reading the papers, if he hadn't already, he'd discover what was going on. 'My mother is…an alcoholic. My father has finally installed his mistress in the house and my mother tried to drown herself in drink.'

'Oh, Daisy. Is that what you couldn't tell me?' He cupped her face and kissed her. 'Did you think I wouldn't understand?'

She kissed him back but then slowly shook her head. 'I ruined our family's reputation once before. I couldn't do it again.'

'I don't understand. How did you ruin the reputation of your family?'

'In my final year of med school, I met a guy called Walter. We hit it off right away and we fell in love, or so I thought.' She sighed and shook her head sadly.

'He turned out to be someone different?'

'In a way. He turned out to be someone who wasn't past trying to make some money selling a story to the papers.'

'Ah.' It all made sense now. 'You told him about your mother,' he stated and she nodded.

'Walter and I had been together for five months, we'd planned to get married and he'd given me a toy ring from a vending machine as a makeshift engagement ring.' She smiled at the memory. 'I'd loved it because it wasn't flash or an enormous diamond. It was…fun.'

'Did you bring him home?'

'To meet my father. Yes. He insisted on doing everything right. Asking my father's permission to marry, meeting my mother, becoming best friends with my brother. He was eager to please.'

'Did he know who your family was before you met?'

'I don't know.' The smile slipped from her face and she

shrugged. 'Still to this day, I don't know if he targeted me or not. My father said he must have because when Walter discovered my mother was a recovering alcoholic, he didn't hesitate to try and sell the story to the highest bidder.'

'What happened then?'

'My father has spies everywhere. Especially at different newspapers. He got wind of the story and paid Walter off. Walter received more money than he could ever have hoped for and completely disappeared from my life.'

'And your father blamed you for the entire thing? For "ruining the family"?'

'Yes, but he also emotionally abused my mother for a long time after that. He said that if she hadn't been drinking, Walter never would have had a story to sell. He calls her a disgrace. He berates her and criticises her at every opportunity.' She was gritting her teeth again and he could quite clearly hear the disgust in her tone. 'He kept everything out of the papers and still ensures that his PR team handle anything and everything to do with information about the family.'

'So why wasn't he able to stop it this time?'

'Because he didn't want to, because he wants my mother to be disgraced, to paint her as the reason he wants to divorce her and marry his mistress.'

Oscar shook his head in disgust. He could see how upset Daisy was and he knew that no matter what happened between them, he needed to tell her the truth, to be completely honest with her.

'I have to confess I did try to look you up online and, apart from some very flattering pictures of you dressed in your army uniform and one of you in a very flash ball gown when you were younger, there really isn't that much about you I didn't already know.'

'You looked me up online?'

Was that disgust or disbelief in her tone? 'You weren't giving me *any* information, Daisy. I wasn't sure if your mother had passed away or whether you were still safe. I was beside myself with worry. I had to do *something*.'

'I thought you'd be angry with me.'

'I was. I still am. Very angry. Don't you ever try and cut me out of your life like that again because I will find my way back into that inner sanctum you keep so tightly locked up.'

'Giving me orders, Dr Price?'

'No, Major Forsythe-York. Making you a promise.' He leaned over and kissed her, wanting her to feel, rather than rely on his words, just how much he adored her. When they broke apart their breathing was ragged. 'I've missed you so much,' he whispered against her lips before kissing them once more. A moment later, she pulled back and looked at him. 'Wait a second. How could you leave Meeraji Lake? Who's looking after the patients?'

'Tori found a locum. Her name is Harriette and she's happy to stay there for at least the next twelve months.'

'Oh? Well, that's good news, for the town. I do miss everyone. Oh, how are Scotty and Tori? Back together, I hope.'

He smiled and nodded. 'They are. And now *we're* back together because, crazy woman, I'm not letting you go, ever again.'

'Wait. Wait. Are you saying that…you're staying? Here? In England? With me?'

He tightened his grip around her and dropped a kiss to her nose. 'That's what boyfriends do.'

'Boyfriend?' She giggled nervously at the word. 'You're my boyfriend?'

'Yes.' He grinned, loving her reaction.

'Do I get a say in this?'

'No.'

'Oh.'

'Got a problem with that, Your Ladyship?'

'If I do, am I allowed to register a complaint?'

'No.'

Daisy smiled, then kissed him soundly on the lips. 'You are amazing.'

'I love you, Daisy. That's the amazing thing. I never thought I'd feel this way again and this time, with you, everything is magnified. Where I thought I was happy before, I'm ecstatic now.'

'Oscar, I—'

'You don't have to reply. I'm not trying to put you on the spot. I'm here for you, Daisy. I think you don't really know what it's like to be loved so I'm going to give you very clear examples of what that means.'

'Like travelling halfway around the world to support me?'

'Exactly. See, you're a fast learner.' He kissed her and she responded with such abandonment, as though she was trying to express the way he made her feel with actions because she wasn't sure how else to show him.

After a moment, he drew back, both of them breathless and filled with desire. 'Perhaps this isn't the best room in the house to have a reunion.'

Daisy nodded, overcome with emotion. Her lower lip began to wobble. 'Thank you. Thank you so much, Oscar. Thank you for coming, thank you for pushing through my stubbornness, thank you for…for…loving me.' She started to choke back the tears but Oscar shook his head.

'Let it out, Daisy. You've been carrying far too much on your shoulders. Together we'll deal with this.'

'How?' She sobbed.

'Well, why don't we take your mother someplace else?

Somewhere she likes. Perhaps your mother will finally be ready to leave him.'

'I hope so. Will you come and talk to her with me? Help me to convince her? Is that sort of thing part of the boyfriend description?' She pulled back and looked at him, hope in her eyes.

He smiled warmly. 'Of course it is.'

Daisy thought for a moment, then nodded slowly. 'She likes Spain.'

'Then Spain it is. We'll rent a place where the three of us can relax and talk and find some sort of peace.'

More tears gathered in her eyes. 'Is this what love is? Being kind? Thinking of others? Being supportive?'

'And all of it completely unconditional.'

'Oh, Oscar. If that's true, then I love you. I love you so incredibly much that it feels as though my heart is going to break through my chest.'

He brushed the loose tendrils of hair back from her face and kissed her lips. 'Mine, too. I love you, my beautiful Daisy. You've brought so much sunshine to my life and I hope you continue to do so forever.'

She nodded earnestly. 'Yes. Yes, I will. It won't be easy, Oscar. You know that, don't you? My family is—'

'Your family is *me*. And Tori and Scotty and Glenys and Erica,' he added. 'And all of the Meeraji Lake district.'

'And my mother?'

He nodded. 'Let's hope so.'

Daisy smiled and kissed him. 'I'm liking the sound of this love thing, this family thing…this you-and-me thing.'

'Do you think "this you-and-me thing" might end with a wedding?'

Daisy couldn't help but laugh, a rich sound of pure happiness. 'Oh, it had better because now that I've found you, Dr Price, there's no way I'm ever letting you go.'

'I like the sound of that, Dr Daisy.'

Then he stood and gathered her to him once more, kissing her soundly, both of them more happy than they could ever have imagined.

EPILOGUE

DAISY AND OSCAR stood barefoot on the beach in Spain in the cool of the day, a small marquee erected over their heads. Scotty stood beside Oscar as his best man and Tori stood beside Daisy as her maid of honour. Daisy's mother sat in a wheelchair on the other side of her daughter, the two of them holding hands.

It was far more than Daisy could ever have dreamed. For the past eight weeks, she had come to know her mother as she'd never thought possible. There had been no objection from her father or her brother when she'd told them she was taking her mother to Spain. In fact, her brother had seemed more relaxed at this news as it meant he would no longer be hounded by reporters.

Thankfully, Cecilia had finally realised that the life she was living was no life at all and that she did deserve better. In Spain, her mother had relaxed more and, through Oscar's coaxing and relaxed Aussie manner, had started to open up, just as Daisy had. The two women had talked and cried for past hurts and lost opportunities.

'Oscar is an absolute delight,' her mother had said just that morning. 'At first I thought him rather rustic and uncouth but now I understand. I most definitely see the appeal and I could not be happier that it is *him* you are marrying.'

'Thank you, Mother.'

Her mother had become rather emotional then but, rather than shying away from her emotion, she embraced it and held Daisy's hand in hers. 'I've never said this before and it's long past overdue but I'm so proud of you, Daisy. You have done things I did not have the courage to do. You have stood your ground, gone head to head with your father and shown him that you cannot be bullied. And now look at you. You are so beautiful. A bride, waiting to be united with her knight in shining armour.'

Daisy had had a difficult time choking back the tears. 'Oh, Mother. Thank you.'

'And Oscar said that if I continue to improve, I'll be able to return to Meeraji Lake with you.' Cecilia said the town's name slowly and carefully as though she'd been practising it. 'After all, if I'm going to be a grandmama in the future—a real one, who plays with her grandchildren and feeds them lots of sugary stuff and buys them too many toys—then I need to get better.'

'Of course you do.' Daisy had laughed through her tears and hugged her mother close. 'I love you, Mother.'

'Oh. Oh.' The two women had been choked up, those very precious words never having been expressed between them before. 'Well. Well, then.' Speech had been difficult for a moment and when Cecilia had looked at her, she'd shaken her head. 'Daisy, you'll need to redo your make-up if you don't start to control those tear ducts.'

Daisy knew that haughtiness was a front for feeling uncomfortable and she laughed once more. 'Then I'll redo it. Moments like this don't happen every day.'

And neither did standing beneath the marquee with the man of her dreams looking at her as though she were the most precious, most wonderful, most incredible person in the world. What she'd done to deserve a man like Oscar, she had no clue, but there was no way she was going to let him go now. She knew he missed his life in Meeraji Lake and so did she. After all, it really was their home.

Now, as they stood before the celebrant, they held hands and looked into each other's eyes. 'There are so many things I want to say to you,' Oscar began. 'But I've realised that I have the rest of my life to say them, to show you how incredibly happy you've made me. I never thought I'd find love again but I was wrong. For a long time, I wasn't sure if you were Major Daisy, Dr Daisy or Lady Daisy, but now I know, with one hundred per cent clarity, exactly who you are—you're *my* Daisy and I promise to love you forever. Work beside me. Walk beside me. Communicate with me. Laugh with me. Cry with me. Listen with me… and I promise to do the same, with all my heart.'

Daisy's lower lip had started to wobble as he'd spoken and she sniffed and quickly looked at her mother. 'I may need to redo my make-up yet again.' They all laughed but then she turned her full attention to the man before her, her heart swelling with a love she'd never known possible but was more than happy to accept.

'Oscar.' She gave his hands a little squeeze and he immediately smiled at her. 'I *love* you.' She paused. 'It really is that simple. I *love* you and I have never loved anyone until you. Because of you, I can now love others.' She smiled at her mother and then at Scotty and Tori, so pleased their two friends had been able to travel to Spain to be here for their special day. 'You have given me so much and I want nothing more than to make you happy. Thank you for saving me.'

Oscar gathered her close. 'It has been my absolute pleasure.' Then he kissed her, even though they weren't really up to that part in the ceremony yet. No one seemed to mind, though. This was their day and they could do whatever they wanted.

* * * * *

Look out for the next great story in
Lucy Clarke's OUTBACK SURGEONS *duet*
A FAMILY FOR CHLOE

And if you enjoyed this story,
check out these other great reads
from Lucy Clark

STILL MARRIED TO HER EX!
A CHILD TO BIND THEM
DR PERFECT ON HER DOORSTEP
HIS DIAMOND LIKE NO OTHER

Available now!

MILLS & BOON®
Hardback – May 2016

ROMANCE

Morelli's Mistress	Anne Mather
A Tycoon to Be Reckoned With	Julia James
Billionaire Without a Past	Carol Marinelli
The Shock Cassano Baby	Andie Brock
The Most Scandalous Ravensdale	Melanie Milburne
The Sheikh's Last Mistress	Rachael Thomas
Claiming the Royal Innocent	Jennifer Hayward
Kept at the Argentine's Command	Lucy Ellis
The Billionaire Who Saw Her Beauty	Rebecca Winters
In the Boss's Castle	Jessica Gilmore
One Week with the French Tycoon	Christy McKellen
Rafael's Contract Bride	Nina Milne
Tempted by Hollywood's Top Doc	Louisa George
Perfect Rivals...	Amy Ruttan
English Rose in the Outback	Lucy Clark
A Family for Chloe	Lucy Clark
The Doctor's Baby Secret	Scarlet Wilson
Married for the Boss's Baby	Susan Carlisle
Twins for the Texan	Charlene Sands
Secret Baby Scandal	Joanne Rock

MILLS & BOON®
Large Print – May 2016

ROMANCE

The Queen's New Year Secret	Maisey Yates
Wearing the De Angelis Ring	Cathy Williams
The Cost of the Forbidden	Carol Marinelli
Mistress of His Revenge	Chantelle Shaw
Theseus Discovers His Heir	Michelle Smart
The Marriage He Must Keep	Dani Collins
Awakening the Ravensdale Heiress	Melanie Milburne
His Princess of Convenience	Rebecca Winters
Holiday with the Millionaire	Scarlet Wilson
The Husband She'd Never Met	Barbara Hannay
Unlocking Her Boss's Heart	Christy McKellen

HISTORICAL

In Debt to the Earl	Elizabeth Rolls
Rake Most Likely to Seduce	Bronwyn Scott
The Captain and His Innocent	Lucy Ashford
Scoundrel of Dunborough	Margaret Moore
One Night with the Viking	Harper St. George

MEDICAL

A Touch of Christmas Magic	Scarlet Wilson
Her Christmas Baby Bump	Robin Gianna
Winter Wedding in Vegas	Janice Lynn
One Night Before Christmas	Susan Carlisle
A December to Remember	Sue MacKay
A Father This Christmas?	Louisa Heaton

MILLS & BOON®
Hardback – June 2016

ROMANCE

Bought for the Greek's Revenge	Lynne Graham
An Heir to Make a Marriage	Abby Green
The Greek's Nine-Month Redemption	Maisey Yates
Expecting a Royal Scandal	Caitlin Crews
Return of the Untamed Billionaire	Carol Marinelli
Signed Over to Santino	Maya Blake
Wedded, Bedded, Betrayed	Michelle Smart
The Surprise Conti Child	Tara Pammi
The Greek's Nine-Month Surprise	Jennifer Faye
A Baby to Save Their Marriage	Scarlet Wilson
Stranded with Her Rescuer	Nikki Logan
Expecting the Fellani Heir	Lucy Gordon
The Prince and the Midwife	Robin Gianna
His Pregnant Sleeping Beauty	Lynne Marshall
One Night, Twin Consequences	Annie O'Neil
Twin Surprise for the Single Doc	Susanne Hampton
The Doctor's Forbidden Fling	Karin Baine
The Army Doc's Secret Wife	Charlotte Hawkes
A Pregnancy Scandal	Kat Cantrell
A Bride for the Boss	Maureen Child

MILLS & BOON®
Large Print – June 2016

ROMANCE

Leonetti's Housekeeper Bride	Lynne Graham
The Surprise De Angelis Baby	Cathy Williams
Castelli's Virgin Widow	Caitlin Crews
The Consequence He Must Claim	Dani Collins
Helios Crowns His Mistress	Michelle Smart
Illicit Night with the Greek	Susanna Carr
The Sheikh's Pregnant Prisoner	Tara Pammi
Saved by the CEO	Barbara Wallace
Pregnant with a Royal Baby!	Susan Meier
A Deal to Mend Their Marriage	Michelle Douglas
Swept into the Rich Man's World	Katrina Cudmore

HISTORICAL

Marriage Made in Rebellion	Sophia James
A Too Convenient Marriage	Georgie Lee
Redemption of the Rake	Elizabeth Beacon
Saving Marina	Lauri Robinson
The Notorious Countess	Liz Tyner

MEDICAL

Playboy Doc's Mistletoe Kiss	Tina Beckett
Her Doctor's Christmas Proposal	Louisa George
From Christmas to Forever?	Marion Lennox
A Mummy to Make Christmas	Susanne Hampton
Miracle Under the Mistletoe	Jennifer Taylor
His Christmas Bride-to-Be	Abigail Gordon